Volume Two

Episode Three
The Ransom of Renaissance

Episode Four
Conflict on Cada-Maylon

PRESS

OWL and BOWL Press

Dedication

This new version of the Zaanan books episode three and episode four is dedicated to my parents Henry and Auline Bohl. All they ever tried to do was teach me how to be a good person. They lived long enough to see the positive results of their selfless labors. The book is also dedicated to my sisters Candace Crow and Donita Barnwell. I love you both and I'm honored to be your brother.

Acknowledgement

I gratefully acknowledge **Hugh Barbour** for not only giving me a chance by publishing the first four Zaanan books but for being willing to give it all back to me years ago. You have always treated me with professionalism and integrity. Thank you.

Episodes Three: The Ransom of Renaissance and Episode Four: Conflict on Cada Maylon were published by Barbour and Company as part of their "Young Readers Christian Library." All rights were returned to Al Bohl to republish as desired as long as the format of the books was different from the original size and style of the first books.

Cover art by James Hislope

TERMS AND PEOPLE YOU WILL READ ABOUT

Alien-thought - Any idea, religion, or movement contrary to Sphere.

Allison - Well-known artist of Sphere.

Asaph - Senior leader of a rebel space colony.

Baron - Military athlete and father of Zaanan.

Edolf - Leader of the terrorist Planetarians.

Fatal Limit - A nuclear waste dump in outer Space. Christians found a way to recycle the waste and use the Limit to power and conceal their Space Colony.

Calvert Van Hensen - Zaanan's superior officer.

Holocaust - Nuclear world war in the twenty-fifth century.

Joseph - Zaanan's twin brother.

Kara - Medical research scientist and mother of Zaanan.

Malcolm - Head of Sphere's Secret Police (SSP).

Maroth - Absolute ruler of Troz.

Normals - Regular Sphere Police Force.

Power arms - Pair of metallic gloves used for protection and communication only by Talgents warriors; powered by nuclear fusion.

ZAANAN
Episode Three: The Ransom of Renaissance

Chapter One

Holocaust Year: A.D. 2453
Present Earth Year: A.D. 3007
Year of Sphere: 554

Location: Leadership conference center in the City of Sphere.

"For there is one God and one mediator between God and men, the man Christ Jesus, who gave himself as a ransom for all men."

1 Timothy 2:5, 6 NIV

Phtoom!

"Runnlings," whispered Calvert Van Hensen to Malcolm.

4

Malcolm acted as though he didn't hear the Calvert. Another blast of fireworks lit up the sky. Malcolm didn't flinch.

"You still haven't caught up with the runnlings, have you, Malcolm?" pressed Calvert Van Hensen.

This was a slap in Malcolm's arrogant face.

Malcolm was the decorated leader of the merciless and ruthless SSP, the Sphere Secret Police. He was the most feared, most bitter man in sphere. Another firework danced on the black night sky. Van Hensen could barely contain the wail of laughter he so wanted to express. He coughed trying to hide it. Other leaders nearby had witnessed the Calvert's dig, and they too suppressed their amusement. Several fireworks could now be seen exploding outside the giant windows that made up the walls of the Leadership Conference Center. Unable to contain themselves, several tables of men in that section of the center burst into laughter.

Everyone except Malcolm. He whirled around and flashed

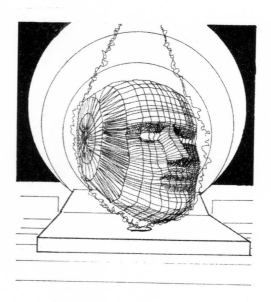

an evil glare that instantly sobered up everyone but Calvert Van Hensen. Malcolm leaned over, his face reddened, and the veins on his neck began to show in anger. The Calvert stopped laughing. Suddenly he couldn't find a comfortable position in his seat. Malcolm's face turned shades of red as he searched his mind for just the right words to blast the Calvert.

Down in the front of the auditorium, at center stage, a three-dimensional face began to form. Its features were strong, sharp - but the eyes could barely be distinguished. Everyone's attention was swiftly turned to the face of Sphere. Everyone's except Malcolm's - he leaned over and stared at Calvert Van Hensen.

"Later," Malcolm said softly but sternly as he turned his attention toward the Sphere image. The entire assembly rose to its feet and applauded. A meeting such as this was rare.

"Sit," said the face. Everyone complied. "I am gravely concerned over the apathy of our citizenry," began the Sphere. "Holidays appear to mean nothing. Work production is dwindling, and

diary entries are shamefully sloppy. More and more of our people are defecting to splinter groups that lure them with alien-thought. My deepest concern is over the rising disappearance of infants and the elderly. Effective today, every Sphere citizen will go through our history course again. This course will require their coming to work one hour earlier."

Everyone human at the meeting wanted to groan, but didn't dare. Each adult citizen of Sphere already worked two eight-hour jobs each day. A diary of what happened during their jobs had to be logged before they went to their next job or home.

"Also, each person will begin turning in a diary report through the Chron about what they do in their seven hours of free time. I've designed some new technology to examine their diaries. It is very sensitive to any wording that may reflect any alien-thought." One of the leaders rose to her feet and raised her hand.

"Do you wish to speak?"

"Yes," she said politely. "I feel that I can speak for most of us here and say that the people we lead already feel overworked.

We only hear complaints about diary logging. More free time and less diary requirements would produce a more positive outlook and sincere loyalty."

"Silence!" thundered the Sphere image. The leader took her seat quietly. "Does everyone truly feel as she does?" No one moved a muscle on her behalf.

"Daily the environment of this planet is getting more and more out of control. I work constantly cleaning the air, improving nutrition, and attempting to stabilize the weather. I do not want advice from you; I demand obedience. I allow you an opportunity to lead, and I only receive complaints. Obey my directive and stop alien-thought."

The face disappeared as quickly as it had come. For a long moment, no one moved. Then one by one the assembly sheepishly left the meeting hall.

"Malcolm," said a tiny voice inside a monitor on his desk in the meeting hall.

"Yes," said Malcolm, sitting back down.

"I want her diary entries for the past ten years rechecked, and I want her questioned thoroughly about any oddity," directed the Sphere main computer. The Sphere had recently determined that the upgrades to the main computer had moved the main brain to an advanced level and determined it would be better described as

the Coreum.

"Yes. Right away," said Malcolm. "I have an idea I'd like your permission to pursue. It's about the missing infants and elderly."

"Permission granted," answered the Sphere computer, ending the transmission.

In a moment, Malcolm had the director of testing on visual display monitor at his conference desk.

"Is anyone taking the life extension test right now?" asked Malcolm.

"Yes, sir. Most are age fifty-five and passing."

''Is anyone failing the test, or at least sixty years old?" quizzed Malcolm.

''Yes, sir. We have a man of sixty-two who should pass the exam," said the director.

"Prolong his testing until I arrive," instructed Malcolm.

Malcolm ended his conversation with the director and rose from his desk to leave. He looked for Calvert Van Hensen, who had long since departed, "Well, the great Calvert didn't wait for me," he laughed to himself. "We'll meet again. I never break a promise."

Chapter Two

The test for life extension was given in the same complex of buildings as the meeting hall. Malcolm was in the testing center in moments. The director of testing was waiting at attention as Malcolm and his aide Thwart marched in.

"Where is the man you spoke of?" asked Malcolm impatiently. "He is in the physical portion of the test now, examination room 317," replied the director.

At age fifty-five everyone in Sphere began a series of tests to determine their value to society. They were given mental, emotional, and physical tests. A failure in only one of the three meant complete failure and the sleep injection. Later the people were frozen and stored. As younger citizens of Sphere became ill and

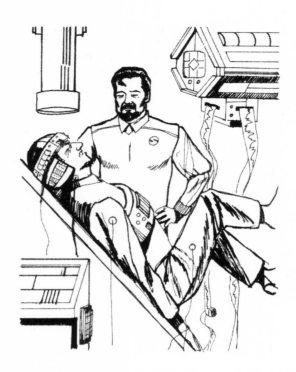

needed an organ transplant, these frozen people would act as
donors. Should a person pass all three tests, he or she was given a
life extension until the following year. Each year the test became
harder, in order to force failure. The older a person became the
more stressed and fearful they were of the test.

"Hello, Jameston," said Malcolm as he breezed into the examination room. "How are you feeling?"

Jameston was trying so hard to maintain his level of effort that
he didn't answer. He was strapped to a table that was tilted at an
angle. Only his legs and feet were free to move during this test.
Malcolm passed his hand over a lighted dot on the table's edge.
The machine stopped.

"Jameston, I'm afraid I have bad news for you," began Malcolm.

"What?" said Jameston, suddenly nervous. He was already
sweating a great deal.

"You failed the written test, so we're stopping your testing.

Go home, and get things in order, and report to the Sleep Center for the sleep injection," said Malcolm, with no emotion in his voice.

All the color drained from Jameston's face as the attendants removed the monitor probes and straps from his body. The table reclined to a flat position. He didn't sit up. He just stared at the ceiling above him.

"It's a shame, too," began Malcolm, standing beside him. "You failed by such a small error. Your record of loyalty to Sphere makes it even more of a shame."

Jameston tried to choke back the tears, but he couldn't. He put his left hand over his face and sobbed uncontrollably.

"Of course, I've never had the sleep injection, but I'm told it isn't very painful. My major problem with the process is that it takes so long to give the shot. However, when you compare it to the bliss of sleep, it's nothing," Malcolm said flatly.

Jameston reached over for Malcolm in a pleading manner. "Please, is there something I can do?"

"I'm sorry. I truly am," confided Malcolm insincerely.

13

"I'll do anything," Jameston begged.

"Would everyone excuse us for a moment?" Malcolm asked. "I need to talk to Jameston." Everyone left the room except Malcolm and Thwart. "You said you would do anything."

"Yes, sir. Anything to live," Jameston said, sitting up.

Malcolm walked over to a window and looked outside for a moment. Jameston and Thwart followed his every move with their eyes as he acted as if he were trying to come to a decision.

"How would you like a life extension until you die of natural causes at a very old age?" Malcolm asked.

"Yes. I'd do anything for that," answered Jameston.

"I know of a secret mission for Sphere that is very dangerous, and you just might be our man," toyed Malcolm. "Everyday Sphere is losing elderly people and tiny babies. Someone - some group - is kidnapping them. We're afraid for their safety. Your job would not be to stop them, but rather to find them and report back to us. We would come pick you up and catch the criminals." Malcolm walked back to Jameston and placed both hands on his shoulders. "What do you say?"

"I'll ... I'll do it," Jameston replied. "Anything for Sphere."

"Good," said Malcolm, gleefully shaking Jameston's hand. "Now

14

you go back to your living quarters and wait. Hopefully you'll be contacted and taken. Don't try to notify us until you find their hideaway. Do you understand?"

"Yes, sir," answered Jameston.

"One final thing before you go," said Malcolm, lowering his voice for emphasis. "Should you double cross us, remember that we will find you and you will pay with a slow, painful price. Do we understand each other?"

"Yes, sir. I understand."

"Good. You may leave."

Jameston acted like a new man as he left the room for home.

"I didn't realize that you have the power to give life extensions like that," said Thwart.

"I don't," said Malcolm with a cold smile. "I said he could die of natural causes at an old age.

15

His file now says that he failed the test. What could be more natural than the sleep injection for that old fossil? Hopefully, his life will extend long enough to help us."

Jameston took the monorail back to his quarters to sleep the remainder of the night. He was awakened by two men, dressed in all black clothing, standing beside his bed. They wore dark cloth masks with holes for their eyes and mouths. Jameston was startled as he sat up.

"We are friends," assured one of the men. "Are you Jameston X5 TRZ 14-6? Are you scheduled to receive the sleep injection in the morning?"

"Yes, I'm Jameston," he replied.

''We can help you escape to live a natural life span, if you like," said the same man, who was still partially hidden in the room's shadows.

"How can you do this? I don't have anything to repay you with," said Jameston.

"Something isn't right here," said the other masked man.

"What do you mean?" retorted the first man. "Have you ever seen a person scheduled for the sleep injection actually sleep the

16

night before?''

"No, I haven't," agreed the leader.

"I took some medication to calm me. They - they gave it to me at the Testing Center. They said it was new. I was going to run away in the morning, anyway. I had it all planned. If you can help me, please do!" pleaded Jameston.

"I still don't like it," insisted the masked helper.

"You've been at this too long," said the leader.

"Please take me! I'll do anything. Don't let them put me through the sleep injection! Please, I beg you," implored Jameston, still sitting up in his bed.

"Come on, let's help the old man," said the masked leader.

"'All right," agreed his helper, after studying Jameston's poorly lit face.

"You must leave everything and come at once with us. We have to cover your face and put you to sleep."

Jameston quickly agreed to all their terms. They put a sack over his head. The masked leader took a small metal spray can

17

from his belt and sprayed a fine mist up under the sack. Jameston immediately felt dizzy and sleepy. His kidnappers' voices were muffled and sounded very far away.

Jameston awakened with a start. He sat up refreshed and looked around him. He was aboard some sort of craft. He couldn't be certain, but it seemed like a spacecraft. He was in a large cargo area with elderly people all around him.

"How are you feeling?" asked a young man. "Can I get you something to eat or drink?"

Jameston recognized the man's voice as one of the masked men in his living quarters.

"I'm fine," he replied, still surveying his fellow passengers.

"Who are all these people?"

"They are people like you - ones the Sphere society decided to throw away," said the young man, who was also looking around the room. "We have another area with a few infants in it. Have you ever seen a baby human?"

18

Jameston thought for a moment and realized that he had never seen a baby. Sphere separated parents and babies at birth. Children were put in different nurseries and reared with other children their age by adult supervisors and robots. His childhood was so mundane and structured that he had let most memories of it slip away.

"No, I've never seen a baby. I'm sure of it," he replied.

"Come. There's nothing like it," suggested the young man. He led Jameston to the next cargo section. In a moment they were standing next to a makeshift crib. A baby started gurgling, smiling, and kicking when they looked over into the crib. Jameston couldn't believe his eyes. The baby was so tiny and beautiful. He was speechless with awe.

"This baby was about to be given the sleep injection," his guide said.

"Why?"

"Well, the Genetic Birth Division said that testing at birth showed this baby had flat feet. He was bred for military service and wouldn't have made the grade. I don't understand a society

that throws away babies or old people." The young man noticed Jameston's fixed gaze on the baby. "Would you like to hold him?"

"I don't know. Could I?"

"Certainly. Just support his head and back." Something happened to Jameston's heart as the young man handed him the baby. Feelings he had never experienced before rushed in.

''Can I hold him a moment longer?"

"Yes. Sure," answered the young man. "In fact, babies need to be held. Hold them all, if you want. Just be careful. Of course, where we're going, they will get all the love and attention they need. But then, so will you."

"Where are we going?" Jameston asked as the young man reached the door.

"To a place of new beginnings. The Fatal Limit."

''The Fatal Limit,'' J ameston said to himself as he gently placed the baby back in the crib. He watched the baby and wondered which feeling was stronger in him - the love he felt or his fear of Malcolm.

Chapter Three

''Fatal Limit, calling the Fatal Limit. This is Zaanan calling the Fatal Limit.''

Zaanan hovered in outer space in his starjet. His flight instruments indicated that a colossal field of deadly radiation was just ahead of him.

"The Fatal Limit is somewhere in that nuclear waste dump, but I don't see a safe way in or out," Zaanan said to himself. He had hidden a homing device inside the space colony during an earlier visit. It had easily led him back, but now the trail seemed to have ended. Zaanan made sure his controls were secure and went to the rear of his starjet to check on his father.

Baron had been given the sleep injection months before. Zaanan hoped that possibly the Christians, who lived in the Fatal Limit,

could help revive him. Zaanan couldn't believe that he was this
close to his father and yet so far away. He remembered back
to his childhood in the military nursery program. He would
lie awake at night in his dormitory, thinking of his parents. He
would wonder where they were and if they ever wondered where
he was. Zaanan's recurring dream was that they would one day
live as a family. This desire puzzled him, because no one in his
society had lived as a family in the last five hundred years. Odd
as it seemed to him, he still couldn't shake the yearning.

"I've got to get through," he exclaimed out loud. He went
back to his pilot seat and tried again to contact the Fatal Limit.

"We'd better inform Asaph about this," said the space controller inside the Fatal Limit. "We've never had anyone uninvited
knock on our door before. I don't think he's going to believe that
no one's home."

In a moment Asaph was on the visual communicator, respond-
ing to the controller's call. "How can I help you?" Asaph asked
calmly. "Well, there is a Talgent starjet hovering in space on the
outskirts of our nuclear waste border. The pilot says his name is
Zaanan."

"Zaanan? Are you sure?" asked Asaph with great interest.

"Yes, sir. Our scanner shows two life forms aboard. It could
be a trap," cautioned the controller.

"I don't think so. Open communication channels to him. I
want to speak with him," Asaph ordered.

"Yes, sir. Right away," complied the space controller.

"Zaanan, this is Asaph."

"Asaph! I'm glad you answered," said Zaanan, his hoped
renewed.

''Can I come into the Limit?'' "Who is with you, Zaanan?"
"My father."

23

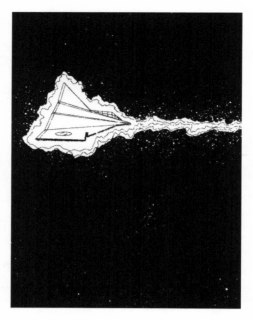

"Baron is with you?" Asaph shouted with joy. "Of course, you may enter. Stay where you are and well send a safety envelope for you."

Moments later, a beam of light from the space colony pierced the darkness. It pushed through the dangerous radiation and engulfed Zaanan's starjet. Zaanan slowly flew his starjet through their nuclear camouflage to the space colony. When he landed in the arrival bay, Asaph was there to greet him. Zaanan jumped from the wing of his starjet to the steel deck.

"It's good to see you again," said Asaph, shaking Zaanan's hand.

"Thank you for letting me through."

''Where is your father?"

"He's asleep," Zaanan answered. "Actually, when I found him, he was in a sleep tube down the throat of an erupting volcano. I rescued him and brought him here. I am in hopes that you can revive him.

"You found him asleep down in a volcano?" Asaph covered his laugh with a cough. "Well, if you went to all that trouble, then certainly we can try to awaken him."

24

Asaph asked some men to carefully remove Zaanan's father from the starjet and take him to the medical center. Asaph glided in his airwalker, and Zaanan walked behind the sleep tube to an elevator.

"You and I can meet up with them in a few minutes. First, we need to talk," Asaph said.

Zaanan agreed, and they moved on to Asaph's study.

"Can you awaken him?" Zaanan asked, getting right to the point.

"To be very honest, I'm not sure," Asaph replied. "As you know, we rescue many elderly people from the sleep center, but so far we haven't kidnapped anyone after they were injected. We've been feverishly working on a dialysis machine that would rid the blood of impurities. If and when this research is successful, we will begin to retrieve people before Sphere has a chance to freeze them."

25

Zaanan became very nervous. His hopes had been high that his father could be helped right away.

"Don't worry, Zaanan, we are very close. You've brought him this far. We must trust that this is part of God's plan," reassured Asaph. "Speaking of God, do you still have the Stone I gave you?"

"Yes," Zaanan said as he checked a secret pocket in his clothing.

The Stone looked like an oblong rock, but in reality, it was a miniature computer, programmed with the Holy Bible. All a user had to do was make a fist around it and ask a question. The Stone had a complete concordance and could recite any related Scripture verses. The sound traveled along the user's skeleton to his eardrum. When the Sphere computer came to power as the one-world government, it tirelessly strove to destroy all written materials. The Holy Bible was at the top of their list. The Christians earnestly asked God what they should do, and in answer to their prayer, they developed the Stone.

26

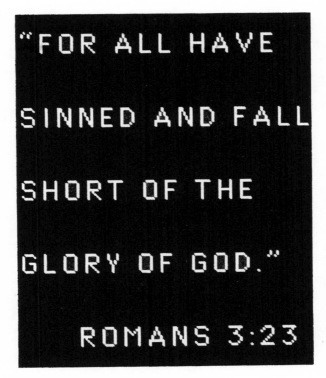

"FOR ALL HAVE SINNED AND FALL SHORT OF THE GLORY OF GOD."

ROMANS 3:23

"Have you used it?" quizzed Asaph.

"Surprisingly enough, I have listened to it often," Zaanan answered. "I've been somewhat amazed at what I've heard. I questioned the Stone about a number of situations. I'm very impressed with what I've heard."

"Good," said Asaph, smiling. "I was hoping that you used it. Do you have any questions?"

They entered Asaph's large study room and sat down by a table.

"Well, there are a lot of things still unclear. For example, what does the word sin mean, and why do these recorders speak as if they know God personally?"

"I think," replied Asaph, "that I can answer both questions by using just four verses from the Stone."

Asaph took his own Stone from a pouch in his robe. He placed it in a special compartment in the conference table. A twelve-inch square screen illuminated in front of Zaanan. Another screen lit

27

up before Asaph.

Asaph said, "Romans 3:23."

The conference table was also a computer. In five seconds, the verse was displayed in writing before both men on the screens.

''For all have sinned and fall short of the glory of God. Romans 3:23," the screen displayed.

"God is holy, pure, almighty and just," explained Asaph. "He has a standard of perfection and holiness that He demands be met. We have all rebelled or chosen our own way over His. This rebellion is called sin. Some people refer to sin as the 'bad things' we do. Here's the next verse. Romans 5:8."

"But God demonstrates his own love for us in this: While we were yet sinners, Christ died for us. Romans 5:8."

This verse displayed on the screen under the first.

"God sent Jesus Christ three thousand years ago to pay the price for sin," said Asaph. "He died a cruel death. He was nailed to wooden beams fastened in the form of a cross. He received

the punishment that you and I deserve. Before you ever sinned, He made a way for you to personally know God. Jesus' death satisfied God's requirement of perfection. Jesus, who was without sin, gave His life in payment for sin. This is love."

Zaanan seemed a little confused by what Asaph was saying.

''Let me give you an example," Asaph continued. "Let's say that a man commits a terrible crime against the Sphere society. Sphere sentences him to Renaissance, the sky prison. This man is guilty and deserves to die for his crime. A completely loyal citizen volunteers out of love to take his place in prison. The law requires that the crime must be punished, so the innocent man becomes the prisoner, and the guilty man is pardoned and set free. Allow me to show the next verse. Romans 6:23."

''For the wages of sin is death, but the gift of God is eternal life in Christ Jesus our Lord. Romans 6:23.''

''Now this verse says that the price for sin is death, or being forever separated from God, but God offers us a free gift of

eternal life with Him. We must accept Jesus' death as the payment for our sin. The prisoner in Renaissance must be willing to let the innocent man take his place. Zaanan, you can't merit it, but you must believe and accept it."

"If you can't earn it, how do you get it?" Zaanan asked, trying to understand.

"Romans 10:13," said Asaph to the Stone. In seconds, the verse took its place under the other three on the screen.
"For everyone who calls on the name of the Lord will be saved. Romans 10:13," read Zaanan out loud.

"You can't earn a relationship with God, but you can receive it by asking for it," said Asaph. "The Stone calls it prayer or talking to God. You must be the one to pray. No one can do it for you."

Zaanan had listened intently and tried to understand, but this was all so foreign to him. In the Sphere society, God was

forbidden. The Sphere computer had directed Zaanan's entire life. In essence, Sphere had been a god to him.

"Perhaps I didn't explain it too well," Asaph said.

"No, you explained it well enough, but I'm not ready to pray or believe anything. I came here because I feel you can help my father and I can trust you."

"Thank you, Zaanan. I appreciate your being honest with me. There is something else I must tell you. A long time ago, your father trusted me with a secret you should know. Sphere selected your parents, Baron and Kara, to have a baby. The baby was to be raised to become a soldier. Your mother became pregnant with you, but also with another baby."

"Two babies? I don't understand what this means?"

Your mother had you and a brother at the same time."

"A brother?"

"Yes, when two are born at the same time, these children are called 'twins.'"

Zaanan sat in his chair, bewildered.

"Sphere ordered Kara to remain pregnant with you but to abort your brother. Your parents were in love and couldn't bear

the thought of killing one of their babies. Because your mother worked in medical research, she was able to trick the computer into thinking she had aborted your brother. She gave birth to both of you in secret. As ordered, you were sent to a military nursery. Your father brought your brother, Joseph, to me to raise."

"I have a twin brother," Zaanan mused to himself.

"Your father and I prayed together years ago that one day you would all live as a family," Asaph said.

Zaanan felt hot tears burn his eyes and a giant lump form in his throat. His training as a warrior wouldn't allow him to release his emotions. He sat uncomfortably silent for a moment, trying to regain control.

"Where is my brother now? I'd like to meet him," he finally said. Asaph stood up and hobbled over to a window that sparkled with an ocean of night stars. "I fear he is in grave danger," he said.

32

"Danger? Isn't he here with you now?"

"He was, until a few days ago. We received word that Malcolm had placed one of our fellow believers in prison. You've met her - Allison."

"Allison!"

"It seems that Malcolm is actually after you.

He thinks you and Allison are romantically involved. He put her in jail thinking you would break Sphere law and rescue her."

"I can't believe this," retorted Zaanan, now on his feet and angry. He walked over and picked up the celuminum sculpture of Allison that he had admired on his first trip to the Limit. Holding the sculpture reminded him once again of her stunning beauty.

"Joseph is in love with Allison." Asaph said. "He has been for a number of years."

Zaanan quickly put the sculpture down and turned toward Asaph.

"When Joseph heard she was in trouble, he shaved off his mustache and foolishly went to her rescue. He has not been on

Earth since he was a very small boy. He is going to try to pass himself off as you."

"I must help them," Zaanan declared as he smashed his fist into the palm of his other hand.

"Don't be rash, Zaanan. If you are caught, Sphere will see your actions as an alien-thought crime," Asaph warned.

"Do you know exactly where they are?"

"We have the plans for the secret police headquarters and know where Allison is. We have no idea where Joseph could be. He left before we received these plans."

"Give me the plans and I'll go after them," Zaanan said as he turned to leave for his starjet.

Asaph handed him a computer disc that contained the information.

Zaanan placed the information in his power arm computer. His right power arm had been damaged when he was down in the volcano rescuing his father, and he hadn't waited to have it repaired before coming to the Fatal Limit.

34

"Zaanan," Asaph called, stopping Zaanan at the door. "God knows our needs even before we ask. I pray that you will see the reality of God in this situation."

Zaanan dashed for his starjet, hoping he wasn't too late.

Chapter Four

Joseph knew that his only hope of landing without immediate arrest was to touch down outside the city of Sphere in an isolated area. He prayed his craft was small enough to slip into the earth's atmosphere undetected. He was wrong. In moments, his small control panel flashed a warning that two objects were approaching him at high rates of speed. He looked out his small window but could see nothing.

"Follow me and don't try to escape," said a voice on Joseph's miniature communicator. A Sphere Air Escort called a Squirt came up in front of Joseph's craft. The other Squirt was behind him. "You are under arrest for illegal entry into Sphere airspace. We will land at the City of Sphere Space Port. Upon landing, do

not disembark from your craft until notified."

Joseph didn't try to escape. He knew he couldn't outrun their
weapons. In a few moments he could see the City of Sphere on
the horizon. It was larger than anything he had ever seen before.
Suddenly, it dawned on him that he had acted foolishly. The
thought of Allison in jail and his twin brother being in love with
her had caused him to misjudge his ability. Here he was in an un-
armed spacecraft, the prisoner of two Squirt jets. Had he reached
Sphere, how would he have found Allison, anyway, or freed her?

He scolded himself and began to pray. "Father, I have acted
foolishly and did not show faith in You. I agree with You that I
have sinned. Please, Father, help me out of this situation. And
please help Allison to escape. In Jesus' name, I pray. Amen."
He looked out a small side window. He had been simply following the Squirt jet. Now close to Sphere, they weren't very high

37

off the ground. Just ahead, between his craft and the outskirts
of the city, lay a gigantic pile of cotton-like clouds. Below the
clouds there appeared to be a swamp or jungle of sorts. The lead
Squirt seemed undeterred by the billowing column of clouds. Joseph began formulating a plan of escape. He hoped, that since he
was in view of the crafts, they were no longer tracking him with
their instruments.

Joseph decided he would wait until the clouds covered the trail-
ing Squirt from his view before making his move. This plan
seemed as foolhardy as his decision to rescue Allison. Once
inside the cloud, he firmly grasped the control levers and positioned himself to see the Squirt behind him. Surprise was the
only thing on his side. Just as he had hoped, the clouds separated
them momentarily. Joseph could feel his muscles tense and his
forehead and palms sweat. The Squirt reappeared as quickly as it
had been covered.

"Next time he's covered, I'm gone." He didn't have to wait long.

They flew into another cloud formation. Unexpectedly the rear Squirt dropped from sight in the cloud. Joseph rolled his craft over upside down and pulled back on his controls. Instead of climbing, he dropped almost straight down. The force welded him to his seat. He couldn't see how far he was above the swamp. He knew that he had to level off close to the ground to keep from being followed.

He had guessed right. The rear Squirt's pilot was relying on his eyes to follow Joseph. The cloud was so thick it took a number of seconds for him to realize that Joseph was no longer in front of him.

Joseph made a backward "C" curl and ended right-side-up again. The swamp was covered in fog. He reversed his engine in an attempt to slow down. His drop from the sky made this almost impossible. He couldn't see the jungle ahead of him because he was blinded by the speed and fog. He was prepared to die, but he certainly didn't want to at the moment. His instrument panel

informed him that he was not far above the surface of the swamp. Dark, gloomy, gray images began to form in the fog in front of him as he feverishly tried to slow his craft.

Ka-whack!

He ran his ship between two trees, knocking off his left and right wings. He prayed that he wouldn't hit a tree head-on. Now he could see a maze of small trees and vines looming in front of him. He couldn't steer away, but when he plowed into the vines, they acted as a giant net. He broke right through them and hit the surface of water.

His angle was such that he skimmed across the top of the water and finally hit a boggy, soft bank. His craft was half in and half out of the water.

The ground was so marshy and wet that the brunt of his crash was absorbed by the swamp's shoreline. He was shaken but un-harmed.

Joseph punched a lever, and his door opened. He could hear monkeys and birds screaming from fear. He crawled out of the

craft into the water and climbed the bank. When he tried to stand,
his legs were so shaky that he collapsed onto the spongy ground.
All his strength seemed to have drained from his body.

As he lay there resting, Joseph noticed that the animals and
birds had become strangely quiet. Then he heard the sound of the
Sphere Squirts, coming in slowly to look for him. They had followed his craft into the foggy swamp by using their radar. They
hovered above the swamp at about thirty feet. Using high-intensi-
ty lights, they searched for his small craft.

Joseph knew that in a moment he would be spotted and captured. His strength was so sapped that he just couldn't move. He
tried to pull himself back into the craft so he could close the door,
but he couldn't.

Out of the fog came a man who looked more like an ape than
a man. The soupy fog and his fatigue made it difficult for Joseph
to see well. The hairy man looked at him and placed a detonator

device inside the spacecraft. Two other hairy men picked up the limp Joseph and carried him into the jungle. The first man closed the door of the craft and followed.

A moment later, the high-beam searchlights from the hovering Squirts fell on the craft. Slowly they began to lower themselves, trying to see if Joseph was still in the craft. With no warning, the detonator went off and blew up Joseph's ship. The hovering Squirts swerved to miss the flying debris. Apparently, they were satisfied that Joseph had been in the craft when it blew up, because they left. The hairy men stood over Joseph. The leader of the group pulled off his hairy covering and revealed that the abundance of hair was a cowl and cloak. Joseph tried to sit up, but fell back, unconscious.

Chapter Five

The fog lifted and sun rays began to filter through the thick jungle like separate shafts of light. The warmth from the sun and its brightness made Joseph squint and cover his eyes as he awoke. He was all alone in the swamp. All was quiet, except for the birds, crickets, and frogs.

He felt something weighing down his feet, raised up slowly, and saw a huge snake slithering across his legs. His heart skipped a beat. The snake continued on its way, as if Joseph were just a log in its path. He thought of his rescuers, but they were nowhere to be found. He had no idea how long he had been unconscious, but he felt stronger. His shoulders were sore from his crash landing.

"Where am I?" he wondered. He climbed a tree and looked in every direction, hoping to get a better perspective of where he was. As he turned around, he saw in the distance the tops of what looked like city buildings, about two or three miles away. He climbed down, checked the position of the sun, and began to walk.

The swamp was difficult to walk through. The mud was so soft that he would sink to his knees in it. The filthy water, waist deep in most places, was sometimes over his head. Briar bushes clawed at his clothing, ripping his shirt and pants legs.

Exhausted, Joseph finally came to a clearing that looked like a well-groomed park. The grass was closely sheared, and the trees well pruned. As he stepped onto the lawn, it felt oddly crisp. He reached down and touched it. The grass was made of a plastic type material. He walked over to a tree - plastic. The park was completely fake. He wondered about the men who had helped him. During his struggle through the swamp, he had kept looking for them, without success. "This is one strange place," he mused

to himself. With the City of Sphere ahead of him, he walked on in the hot afternoon. The sun began to set at around six.

This was the final day of celebration for the Sphere holiday season. These few days of merrymaking were in remembrance of the Sphere computer's or Coreum coming to power after a nuclear holocaust some five hundred years before. Though the festival lasted several days, people only cared about this one day, because most work was halted. People walked the street, relaxed and happy for this small token of freedom. They were all aware that tomorrow they had to go to work an hour earlier.

Joseph had never been to a city before, so he was awed by its size. He immediately noticed that this society was devoid of children. He walked right into the crowd. Two people looked strangely at him and then turned away. He walked past a building with mirrored windows and saw his image. He was filthy. His clothes were torn, and he realized he smelled like the swamp.

45

"Well, so much for blending into the crowd," he told himself.
''Drink cool, refreshing GLEE,'' said a voice above Joseph. A
giant, live-action billboard took up most of the side of a building
across the street. A pretty young girl looked three dimensional on
the screen. She was holding what looked like a soft drink bottle
of green liquid.
"GLEE, a brand-new pleasure sensation that's sure to reward the
happiness of serving Sphere. GLEE, a product of sheer delight,
free for the asking from the pleasure division of Sphere. Come to
a drink station near you. Happy Holocaust Days to you."
Joseph stared at the giant screen as it went blank. In his struggle,
Joseph had forgotten that he hadn't had food or fluids in a good
while. He stepped into the street, moving toward the billboard. A
street tram zoomed past and barely missed him, and he dove for
the sidewalk on the other side. No one helped him up. They just
stared at him.
"This is a different world," he said. Suddenly he was grabbed by
46

the shoulders and pulled to his feet.

"What do you think you're doing?" asked a Sphere Normal policeman. They were called Normals because they were the regular Sphere police.

"Did you just come out of the sewer?" asked the Normal's partner, holding his nose.

Joseph was speechless.

"We're going to have to arrest you."

"Why? What have I done?" Joseph asked hurriedly.

"It's not what you've done. It's more like where you're standing," answered the first Normal. "You're standing on a Sphere emblem."

Joseph looked down and saw that he was standing in a large circle that looked like a stylized letter "S."

"You know, you 're the first guy I ever picked up on this violation," the second man said.

These Sphere emblems were all over the city. Sphere law prohibited anyone from stepping on them, and the purpose was

47

to make sure walking traffic moved in an orderly manner without congestion.

"What's your name?" asked one of the officers.

"Talgent Zaanan," lied Joseph. It turned his stomach to say it, but he felt he had no choice.

"You're a Talgent? Where are your uniform and power arms?" asked the leading Normal.

"What's your code number, Mr. Talgent?" asked the partner.

"Central, this is Normal Hareton. Get me an air wagon down here. We have a real loony for lock up. We're at Section 27, Avenue a-5 in the 42000 block."

Joseph knew he was in trouble and he must not be arrested. One of the officers was speaking with headquarters on his visual communicator, and the other turned toward the live-action billboard as it began advertising the GLEE product again.

Joseph decided he had to make a break for it.

48

He pushed the Normal who was looking at the billboard into his partner and ran.

"Halt or be stunned!" shouted the leader Normal.

Joseph didn't look back as he vaulted into a crowd of people. The Normals fell in behind him, requesting assistance from head-quarters.

Joseph ran as fast as he could for several blocks. His side began to ache from fatigue. He leaned against a wall to catch his breath.

The crowd around Joseph suddenly dropped to the street and the Normals fired at him. The stun ray crashed the brick above his head. He ran again, with the Normals in hot pursuit, ducked into an alley, and ran until he came to a dead end. The alley was dark and creepy, with nothing to climb or hide in. The officers followed him and stopped about twenty yards away, their stun guns aimed at him.

''All right. We can do this the easy way or the hard way," said Normal Hareton.

Joseph raised his hands in surrender and tried to catch his breath.

The officers began cautiously to inch toward him when they suddenly heard a noise behind them.

Joseph heard it, too. A high-pitched giggle echoed off the dark walls of the alley. A hoot like a sick owl came from another area. Next a bloodcurdling scream rang out, followed by several laughing voices.

The Normals forgot all about Joseph and focused their attention on the mysterious noises. Slowly, silently, they backed out of the alley. When they reached the portion of the alley where the streetlights shone, they turned and ran.

Joseph hadn't moved a muscle. He stood with his hands raised near the back wall of the alley. A long period of silence was broken by a giggle, then another. A childlike voice made shrill noises that caused the hair on the back of Joseph's neck to rise.

"The name of the Lord is a strong town; the righteous run to it

50

and are safe," he said, quoting Proverbs 18:10. He didn't feel any safer, In fact, he felt an increasing uneasiness that he was in more danger than he could imagine.

"Trust in the Lord with all your heart and lean not on your own understanding; in all your ways acknowledge him, and he will make your paths straight," quoted Joseph from Proverbs 3:5, 6.

He felt a little better, until he heard multiple voices fiendishly snickering. He decided to try to ease out of the alley. He moved over to the left wall and walked slowly beside it.

An eerie stillness deepened the dark shadows of the alleyway. Joseph kept his eyes wide and jerked his head in the direction of any noise. He was afraid to blink his eyes. He listened so hard that he could almost hear himself sweat.

Something dropped in the dark, then something else. Huge silhouettes began to slowly move toward him.

Joseph turned and stood face-to-face with the enemy. His heart almost stopped beating. The man was shorter than Joseph.

51

He pulled out a laser knife, flicked it on, and slashed it in the air near Joseph's ear and throat.

Joseph swallowed hard and was tempted to see if his throat had been cut.

Next, he felt something sharp touching his back through his torn shirt. He held his breath and arched his back, in an attempt to get away from the laser knife blade. The blade didn't move, and another blade toyed with the hair over his collar.

Joseph wanted to reason with his captors, but couldn't even form any words in his terrified mind.

"Back down," ordered an adolescent voice.

"Come on. Let me zock 'em," pleaded the shorter silhouette in front of Joseph.

"Yea, zock de Bocow," pleaded another, pressing the blade closer to cutting Joseph.

"Zock! Zock! Zock!" chanted voices all around Joseph, growing louder and louder. Silhouettes marched toward him from all directions. "Zock! Zock! Zock!" they cried. Soon the alley was filled with people.

Joseph ignored the temptation to turn around and look at them.

"Me say back down!" ordered Joseph's only ally. Joseph felt the knife in his back disappear.

"Hey, Bocow, what Nermal want?" asked his new friend.

"Nermal?" asked Joseph.

"You be bad Bocow, bad, bad!" laughed the voice.

Joseph checked the silhouette in front of him and slowly turned around. There in a lighted portion of the alley stood a boy about twelve or thirteen years old. As Joseph's eyes adjusted to the shadows, his fear lessened considerably. All around him stood an ocean of children of various ages. He glanced up and saw children hanging from fire escapes and looking out broken windows.

Where did these children come from? he wondered.

"Me say, has you been bad?"

"No, I ... I haven't," answered Joseph.

53

"Me Zock him now?" asked the boy with the laser knife.

"No. What Nermal hate, we like," quipped the leader. "You hate Nermals?"

"I don't hate anyone!" answered Joseph. The crowd took a few steps toward him. "But ... but I don't know them as well as you. My name is Joseph."

"Diljon is me squawk," interjected the leader. "Come, Bocow Joseph." Diljon led Joseph from the alley into an unoccupied building. The entire group broke up, and many followed Joseph. They went through several more ranshacked dwellings and finally into the sewer system of Sphere. Apparently this was their headquarters of sorts, because they stopped and sat down.

Questioning them, Joseph pieced together their origin. Their street language was a simple form of word replacement that was used to help formulate unity in the group. Their grammar showed an almost total lack of formal education. They were a group or gang called the "Runnlings."

These children had escaped from Sphere's nurseries and banded together. They were a constant source of mischief that kept the Normals and Secret Police baffled. These children knew the city and every available hiding place. It was a game to them. This game-like mentality was probably their strongest asset - that and a weapon they called the "Gun."

The children had stolen the gun from a testing laboratory. The authorities knew the children possessed this destructive tool. Yet, the Gun hadn't been used, but their bragging led Joseph to believe that their trigger fingers were itching.

All the gang was dirty, and many were undernourished. Several sitting close by were ill. One young frail girl had a deep hacking cough that seemed to give her pain with each coughing spell. The murky, dank sewer made the dark circles under her empty eyes appear blacker than her eyebrows. Joseph was amazed at how openly they were speaking with him.

"You from Sphere?" Diljon asked.

"No, I'm from a place far away called the Fatal Limit," Joseph explained. "I came here to help a friend who is being held captive by the Sphere Secret Police."

"We halp Bocow," volunteered Diljon. Joseph came to realize that "Bocow" was a name unique to him. One of the Runnlings had made it up on the spot. Joseph explained to them that he didn't see how they could help, since he had no idea where Allison was.

"All I know is that she is being held in a secret prison cell in the SSP headquarters."

All the children laughed, even the sick girl.

"We know all inches of there," squealed Diljon with glee.

"Great. That's wonderful," said Joseph. "But I can't put you in that kind of danger. Show me the way, and I'll . . . "

"Shut face, Bocow," ordered Diljon, standing up and raising his thin arms. All of their pleasant faces turned angry. Joseph saw that their information only came with their help, and he agreed

to let them assist.

"We need something to keep the SSP busy," he suggested.

"Boom, boom," said one of the group. The rest picked up the chant and shouted louder and louder. The children loved the volume and the unity they felt. They chanted for only a few minutes, and then quieted down.

A circle of leadership formed around Joseph. The children, some in their teens, made plans for a diversion and rescue. Joseph was amazed at their genius. Most of the group found a place to lie down and sleep, and Diljon noticed that Joseph was very tired, too.

"Bocow sleep now. We wake in time," Diljon suggested.

Joseph agreed and left the group as they planned on into the night. He found a spot to lie down away from most of the group. The young sick girl he noticed earlier was attempting to sleep about ten yards away. Her entire body shook with each struggle to clear her lungs. Even when she wasn't coughing, her breathing

was labored.

Joseph sat up a moment, taking in all the sights and sounds of his surroundings. His life had been so different. He had been reared in an atmosphere of love and Christlikeness. Now he began to wonder if his trip here was foolhardy or part of God's plan for his life. He watched the sick child struggle to sleep peacefully. He wanted to help her. Other kids were dirty and underfed. He ached to see them enjoy the bounty of the Fatal Limit.

He wanted to share a world of light with them, instead of dark shadows. He wanted to give them his Stone, so they could learn of God. Joseph felt in his pocket and realized his Stone was missing. He reasoned that the men from the swamp must have taken it. He vowed to himself never to go anywhere without Stones to distribute. Finally, he lay down, almost dizzy from the day's adventure. He closed his eyes.

"Help them."

Joseph forced his eyes open, thinking that one of the children must have whispered to him. No one was there. He closed his

eyes. *"Help them,"* the gentle voice said again.

Joseph quickly sat up, but no one around him was awake. He realized it wasn't an audible voice he had heard, but the voice of God's Spirit speaking to his heart. All those years of sitting at Asaph's feet, absorbing the teachings and principles of God, suddenly found a place to serve. The sewer looked different to him, and so did the sleeping children.

Tears welled up in his eyes, and a warmth filled his inner being. "Father, I can't help them, but You can through me. *'Show me Thy ways, teach me Thy paths,'* "he quoted from Psalms 25:4. "I yield to Your will for my life. In the name of Jesus, I will help them. Amen."

Joseph lay back down, physically tired but inwardly empowered.

Just as he was about to drift off to sleep again, he was awakened by noise. He opened his eyes and sat up again. Children from all over the sewer came and lay down around him to sleep.

Chapter Six

"Bocow, it time," said Diljon as he punched Joseph in the side to awaken him. It seemed he had been asleep only seconds. It was three o'clock in the morning. The city slumbered unsuspectingly.

"Gun and Boom-Boom ready for run!" grilled Diljon. "Mojosh, wake every Runnling!"

His right-hand man and others began waking all the children. Joseph's warm feeling was gone now. His stomach felt sour, and his head ached. Even the frail sick girl labored to get to her feet.

"Please stay here and rest," said Joseph after he walked over to her. She was too sick to argue.

"May I pray for you?" Joseph asked. It was apparent that she didn't understand his request. He went ahead and placed his hand on her feverish brow. "Father God, I ask You to heal this little girl in the name and for the glory of Jesus. Amen."

"Now, Bocow. Come now," ordered Diljon as the children began leaving the sewer. Joseph looked back to see the girl lying down with no visible change in her condition.

It was difficult for the children to contain their excitement, but they earnestly tried. They followed the sewer until it came to a fork. There they split into two groups. Joseph stayed with Diljon and Mojosh. All along the way, children broke into small groups and splintered off at each new fork in the sewer system.

"We be here," exclaimed Diljon. He climbed up on the wall of the sewer and grabbed a pipe that ran the length of the sewer system. Clang! Clang! Clang!

Diljon struck the pipe with a steel bar, then placed his ear

61

against the pipe. Down the pipeline he heard a clanging sound that meant his message was received and passed on. Diljon led his group up a rusty ladder to the surface. He pushed back a manhole cover and kept watch as each in his group climbed out and ran into an alley. Joseph had no idea where he was, but the children apparently did. Diljon squinted across a lighted area to a dark building.

"SSP," Mojosh whispered. Joseph looked up at the tall, menacing building. Diljon signaled for everyone to join him. One by one they stole across the lighted street.

"Wait for Gun," ordered Diljon.

On the other side of the building, an officer of the Normal police stood guard. He was very sleepy. A four-year-old Runnling tiptoed over to the glassed front door. She pressed her face to the glass, making an awful face. Then she tapped on the glass.

The Normal looked in disbelief as the little girl stuck out her tongue and ran. The Normal opened the door to see where she

went, only to be jumped and overpowered by ten waiting children.

From the shadows emerged a cannon-like weapon on four
wheels. The children were thrilled at the opportunity to use the
weapon. They weren't sure what it would do, but this only added
to their excitement. They positioned it to fire on the lobby of the
Secret Police Headquarters. Security was low because no one had
ever dared to attack the most feared group in Sphere before.

"Stay clear," ordered the trigger man, who was only ten years
old. Everyone ran for cover.

The boy turned the machine on and pulled the fire lever.

Ka-Boom!

The Gun discharged into the lobby and exploded everything.
It blew a gaping hole right out the back of the building. Diljon's
group was at the side of the building, so no one was hurt. The ten
year old set the Gun on recharge and prepared to fire again.

"Now!" yelled Diljon. They ran into the building using a side

entrance, went through the door to the , and over to the return air vent.

Ka-Boom!

The Gun discharged again, shaking the entire building. Rapidly the headquarters looked like a stirred-up ant farm. Normal and Secret police were caught off guard. They couldn't decide what to do. Half tried to put out fires, and the others prepared to defend themselves.

Children stationed on the roofs of nearby buildings began shooting fireworks at the headquarters. The teenagers pulled the Gun back to a secluded place and joined the fireworks attack.

Diljon, Joseph, and Mojosh started their scramble up the air ducts toward the prison section. Up, up they struggled as carefully and quickly as possible.

Outside, the children still had the police at bay. The Runnlings were more like phantoms. They were positioned in enough places that they never fired from one spot for long.

Malcolm had been notified at his living quarters of the attack. Moments later, he flew to the headquarters roof, using his carcopter. Thwart met him on the roof.

"What's going on here?" shouted Malcolm. "We're under attack!" answered Thwart.

"I know that! Who? Where? And how many are there'?" demanded Malcolm. "We're not sure," Thwart replied as he followed Malcolm into the building. Malcolm went directly to his plush, spacious office.

''Computers on," he ordered as he entered the room. A large black table that hovered in the air lit up. "There must be something in this building that they want," Malcolm reasoned. "Is anyone in the building not wearing a clearance badge?'

Malcolm asked the computer. A diagram of the structure flashed on the giant screen. Three small lights flashed.

"Three humans are inside air ducts of the fifteenth floor," said the computer in a synthetic voice.

"So, just as I suspected, the fireworks were a diversion," Malcolm said.

"Do we stop them?" Thwart asked.

"No. Let's see what they want so badly," Malcolm said as he stood leaning against a large window, watching the fireworks.

Across the street on the roof of a building, Runnlings were firing away. Malcolm could see them from the window.

"Runnlings," he laughed. "Runnlings - kids - are attacking the Sphere Secret Police!" His voice grew louder with each word he spoke. "Only children would be so foolhardy."

Down below, several of the Runnlings had been captured and stunned. Most continued their phantom attack.

"The humans are out of the air ducts now, on the eighteenth floor," informed the computer.

"The secret prison floor," said Malcolm. "Just as I hoped. It's Zaanan. He's fallen into my little trap. He's come to rescue Allison."

Allison was a Sphere artist and an underground Christian. Asaph had asked her to talk to Zaanan and explain what it meant to follow Jesus Christ. Zaanan was instantly attracted to her because of her beauty. Unknown to Zaanan, his twin brother, Joseph, had been in love with Allison for several years. Joseph had wanted to marry her, but she wanted to finish her training as an artist.

Malcolm misunderstood the actual relationship between Zaanan and Allison, thinking they loved each other. Romantic relationships were strictly forbidden in Sphere. Malcolm's personal bitterness toward Zaanan made him want to disgrace Zaanan. Malcolm imprisoned Allison to lure Zaanan into an attempt to rescue her. He felt this would give him enough evidence against Zaanan to show he was disloyal to the Sphere society.

"Come, Thwart. Let's go get them," Malcolm ordered. The taste of what he thought was victory, was sweet to him.

Meanwhile, on the eighteenth floor, Joseph, Diljon, and Mojosh made their way toward Allison's cell. There were a number

of prison cells on that floor, none were lighted.

Outside, the attack was still going on. The police had new officers joining them all the time. More and more children were being taken captive.

"We must hurry," Joseph urged. "The sun will be coming up soon. Let's split up and try each cell."

Diljon waved his hand over a light pad and the door to the cell opened, but it was empty. Joseph tried the next cell with the same result.

''Over here," Mojosh called.
Joseph flew to the opened door. There on a cot, trying to adjust to the light, lay Allison.

"Allison! " Joseph called.

She looked up and saw Joseph. "Zaanan!" she cried. She had never seen Joseph without a mustache, so she mistook him for his twin.

"We've got to get out of here quickly," Joseph urged her.

"No. We can't escape. Get out while you can," Allison cried.

68

"I'm not leaving without you," Joseph said as he helped her to her feet and held her close. She didn't resist his embrace.

"You're both correct!" Malcolm said, standing in the doorway. "You're not leaving, and you can't escape."

Diljon and Mojosh tried to make a run for it, but Malcolm and Thwart grabbed them. The Runnlings fought back and were slapped to the floor.

Joseph dove for Malcolm as he was about to hit Diljon again. The two struggled and battled around the cell. Allison screamed in horror at the display. Malcolm was a trained warrior, but Joseph was fighting from his heart. Finally, Thwart grabbed Joseph from behind and held his arms.

"Run, Diljon!" Joseph shouted as Malcolm pounded Joseph in the face with his ringed fist.

Diljon and Mojosh were bewildered. They didn't know what to do.

"Run!" Joseph cried again, just before Malcolm's fist plowed into his stomach. The children froze.

Allison and the boys wept as they witnessed the beating Joseph took at the fiendish hands of Malcolm and Thwart. Joseph fell to the floor, unconscious, as Malcolm stood over him.

"Well, Zaanan, I never would have thought you'd be so easy to defeat," Malcolm panted.

He reached down and grabbed Joseph by the shirt at his right shoulder. He tried to pick up Joseph's limp body, but Joseph's torn shirt just ripped more.

"Wait a minute, Wait a minute!" Malcolm yelled. "This isn't Zaanan!"

"What do you mean?" Thwart asked. Malcolm bent down and ripped Joseph's shirt, exposing his shoulders. "Look. He has no mark of Sphere!"

Each Sphere citizen was tattooed promptly after birth. The emblem of Sphere was placed on their right shoulders.

"Who is this man?" Malcolm asked.

"Joseph!" Allison whispered. Tears welled up in her eyes as she covered her mouth in shock.

Malcolm grabbed her by the shoulders and pinner her to the wall. "Do you know him?" he demanded. "Who is he?"
She turned her face away.

''Who is he?'' Malcolm shouted. He slapped her face and threw her to the floor next to Joseph. "Tell me, or he dies right now!" He walked over and placed his boot on the throat of the helpless man.

"Joseph. His name is Joseph," Allison cried. "Why does he look like Zaanan?"

"Because they are brothers," she sobbed as she crumpled over Joseph's body.

"Brothers? Zaanan has a brother?" The look on his face showed that he was trying to absorb what having a brother meant. "Does Zaanan know he has a brother?" he asked Allison.

"I ... I don't know. Please don't hurt him anymore," she cried as she held his head in her lap.

Malcolm's mind went to work quickly, trying to work this situation to his advantage. He motioned for Thwart to join him in the hallway.

"Thwart, you and I are the only two in Sphere who know this man isn't Zaanan. Put the boys in the next cell," he ordered. Malcolm and Thwart walked back into the room. Malcolm had a smile on his normally sour face. Thwart wrestled the boys out and into the next cell.

"Well, it looks like you're both in need of some rehabilitation," Malcolm said, rubbing his hands together.

"Please don't hurt him anymore," pleaded Allison as Joseph began to wake up.

"Why, I wouldn't dream of hurting him. Joseph needs to be rested for his trip."

"Trip? What trip?"

"You're both going to a wonderful place that most people of Sphere know nothing about. It's called Renaissance, and Sphere designed it for citizens with special gifts who simply need an attitude adjustment." "Joseph is not a citizen of Sphere," Allison informed him.

"Joseph? I thought you said his name was Zaanan. He looks

72

like Zaanan to me," Malcolm purred.

Thwart returned to the room.

''Thwart, see that Zaanan, here, and Allison are taken to Renaissance right away. I'll make all the arrangements myself," Malcolm ordered.

"Yes, sir," answered Thwart as he helped Joseph to his feet. Allison followed as Thwart half-carried Joseph from the cell.

Chapter Seven

The sun rose, shedding light on the destruction of the SSP headquarters. The city awakened, and the sounds of a new day filled the air. People slowed only briefly as they passed the building, which was being cleaned up. Many Spherites were in such a hurry to be on time for their "new" history class that they simply ignored the disaster.

Relatively few Runnlings were taken prisoner in the riot. They knew that the escape attempt had failed and suspected that Joseph, Diljon, and Mojosh were being held captive. They felt bewildered and weren't sure what to do. They needed a leader.

"This is Starjet 134-J requesting clearance to land," Zaanan said.

''Star jet 134-J, you are cleared for landing in Bay 6-B,'' replied Space Port Control.

Zaanan thought back to the last time he had been given Bay 6-B. He had arrived to a hero's welcome and been given the Sphere Medallion of Valor for something he had never really done. He felt his stomach knot up a bit as he thought about the night he received the medallion. It was a farce. The only good thing about that night was seeing Allison for the first time. She was such a beautiful creature that she turned everyone's head her way. He was shocked to hear that his twin brother Joseph was already in love with her.

Zaanan wondered if he could honestly say he himself was in love with Allison. Love was forbidden in Sphere society. He asked himself if he loved his brother. He couldn't sort out his feelings because such things were all new to him. As he descended into the Sphere Space Port, he thought about God. If he committed his life to Jesus Christ, would he have to denounce his loyalty to Sphere and lose everything he had worked for? He landed in Space Port Bay 6-B.

No one met Zaanan as he climbed out of the star-jet and

walked through the lobby. It was late afternoon. He didn't want to check in or go by his living quarters, because he didn't want to receive any new orders or answer any questions. He definitely didn't want to make any diary entries. The main Sphere Coreum knew that he had landed, but that was all. All the way from the Fatal Limit, he had tried to formulate a plan to get Allison out of prison and find his impulsive twin.

He walked around the city for awhile in the area near the SSP Headquarters, thinking perhaps his brother had lucked out and gotten that far.

"Pss," said a voice from the shadows. Zaanan had been standing on the corner of Sectors 25 and 26 for about half an hour, looking for his brother. He heard the noise, but didn't think it was meant for him, so he ignored it.

''Pss. Bocow. Come,'' insisted the mysterious voice. Zaanan turned to investigate.

"Over here," said the voice, in hushed tones. Zaanan walked over to the shadow and a lad of ten motioned him to follow. Zaanan followed the boy into the alley and into a vacant building.

76

Moments later, without saying another word, they were in the sewer system of Sphere, sloshing along for about a quarter of a mile.

"Hey! Hey! Bocow back," the boy yelled. A large number of Runnlings came around the corner and greeted Zaanan. They were delighted to see him.

"Where Diljon and Mojosh?" they asked.

Zaanan stood speechless as he tried to understand what was happening. They all looked at him as if they knew him. One frail girl ran up to him and took his right hand. She rubbed her face along the back of his hand and hugged his hand and wrist, grinning from ear to ear. Zaanan blinked hard, trying to understand why they all seemed to know him. "Joseph!" he said as it dawned on him. They thought he was Joseph. "No, I'm not Joseph. I'm Zaanan, Joseph's brother!"

"Where Bocow, then?" asked the frail girl.

"I don't know. Was he here?"

"Bocow Joseph here last night," answered the girl.

The children were disappointed that Zaanan wasn't Joseph.

77

They had hoped that Joseph had escaped, bringing Diljon and
Mojosh with him. They had a long conversation there in the
smelly sewer about the events of the night before, telling Zaanan
of their attack on the SSP Headquarters and the disappearance of
Joseph, Diljon, and Mojosh. They felt sure the three of them were
still inside Headquarters. Zaanan paced back and forth, trying to
formulate a plan to rescue them.

    ''You help Diljon and Mojosh, and we help you," offered a
teenager.

    "Agreed," Zaanan replied.

    They spent several hours formulating their attack from the
night before. They reasoned that the SSP would never expect another one so soon. At three in the morning, the Gun fired into the
building again, followed by fireworks.

    The SSP behaved just as it had during the first attack.

    Zaanan entered the building along through its air ducts, but
unlike Joseph, he had the plans that Asaph had given him. He
also had a cloaking device on his power arm to prevent the security system from finding him. Even though he only had his

left power arm with him, it was more than able to protect him. Zaanan knew that even caught off guard, the SP would be quick to suppress the riot. He entered the duct and began his climb, using his power arm to fly whenever possible.

Within moments, he reached the eighteenth floor, carefully opened the air duct vent, and climbed out. He listened for any sign of detection. When he was satisfied that he was alone, he waved his hand over a light panel. The prison door opened. Inside sat the two boys, Diljon and Mojosh. They stood up when they saw Zaanan, but he motioned them to be quiet. They understood and followed him out to the hallway, then climbed into the duct and began their journey out of Headquarters.

Now for Allison and Joseph, Zaanan thought to himself. He walked over to another cell, opened the door, and saw a figure lying on the cot under a blanket.

"Allison. Joseph," he whispered.

Suddenly the covers flew back and Malcom discharged his Stun gun into Zaanan's chest.

Zaanan clutched his chest, his eyes rolled back in his head, and he fell over onto Malcolm.

"Thwart, get him off me!" Malcom ordered his assistant.

"We got him, sir, just like you said we would!" Thwart said as he rolled Zaanan onto the floor.

"I got him, not we, retorted Malcolm as he adjusted his uniform.

"Uh, yes, sir. What do we do now?" Thwart asked.

"Carry him to the interrogation room."

"But sir, that's on the second floor!"

''Well, go get a hover stretcher, and be quick about it,'' Malcolm ordered impatiently. Thwart dashed out of the room to fulfill his master's orders.

Zaanan lay there motionless, but not stiff. His head began to clear a little, but he couldn't move or open his eyes. Almost as swiftly as Thwart left, he was back. He lowered the stretcher to the floor, then reached over to take off Zaanan's power arm.

"Don't. Not unless you want the shock of your life," Malcolm warned him. "Only a Talgent or a trainee knows how to take off

or put on power arms."

Malcolm helped Thwart move Zaanan onto the stretcher. They each grabbed a bar that ran along the sides of the stretcher. Zaanan could feel the stretcher rise and hover, but he still couldn't move. He could hear as they pushed him along the hallway.

Outside, Diljon and Mojosh joined the other Runnlings. The children were so excited that their friends were free. As day dawned, the last Runnling safely entered the smelly sewer system.

Thwart opened the door to the interrogation room.

"What exactly are we going to do?" Zaanan heard him ask Malcolm.

"Well," said Malcolm, "do you recall my saying I would take care of Joseph and Allison?"

"Yes, sir, I do."

"Well, in their paperwork I listed Joseph as Zaanan, so as far as Sphere knows, Zaanan is on his way to Renaissance with Allison."

''What if this Zaanan contacted someone before he came in here tonight?" asked Thwart.

81

"That's a very good question," pondered Malcolm. "I'll check into that later today. This is the only chance I'll get to rid Sphere of Zaanan, and I'm not going to miss it."

They lifted Zaanan onto the interrogation table and strapped him down. He could feel a metal band strapped around his forehead. Zaanan could hear and know everything as it happened to him, but he couldn't even open his eyes or move a muscle. Malcolm apparently didn't realize that Zaanan could hear him, because he spoke to Zaanan as if he were unconscious.

"Zaanan, I don't mind telling you this, but I hate you. I have for a long time now. I should have been given the rank of Talgent, not you. At one time, I think Talgent would have satisfied me, but I now have other plans for Sphere. With you out of the way, it should be much easier. But I don't want to bore you. In my hand is a name tag for you. It says 'Boyette." We're about to extract your thoughts, and even your subconscious mind. Then we'll give you the sleep injection, freeze you, and give you this new name. What do you think of that, old friend?"

Zaanan wanted to grab Malcolm and beat him mercilessly. Instead, his body was a prison.

"Good-bye, Zaanan ... forever!" laughed Malcolm. He left Zaanan and went to the control room.

Seemingly out of nowhere, Asaph came to Zaanan's mind. The last words Asaph had spoken to him were something to the effect that God knows our needs even before we ask. At this point, Zaanan was totally helpless as he heard the mind probe warming up. He decided to pray.

"God, if there is a God, help me. If You are really real, You know I'm about to die. I don't want to die. If You're real, please do something now!"

"I'm starting at Level One," Malcolm informed Thwart. ''We have to take it to Level Five slowly, or we lose everything. At Level Five, we hit this switch and Zaanan's thoughts and subconscious will be ours."

Zaanan felt no difference as levels two and three were reached. The probing machinery whirled louder and louder. At Level Four, the noise increased without any pain.

"Okay. Our instruments say we can proceed to Level Five,"

Malcolm announced with a proud, wild-eyed grimace on his face. "Level Five complete!" screamed Malcolm above the shrill probe.

Krash!

The door to the interrogation room flew open. In ran five Normal policemen and Kara.

"Hold everything! Don't move!" ordered Kara. Malcolm turned around in bewilderment and disbelief.

"What is the meaning of this?" he stormed.

"You are under arrest for the illegal use of the Genetic Birth Division of Sphere and computer fraud," Kara announced. The Normal police stood ready to move.

Malcolm decided to slip the switch on Zaanan, even if it meant no escape for him. He lunged for the switch.

Tis-zear!

Kara discharged her weapon into the probe's instrument panel. Sparks flew everywhere as the noise died down and the probe shut off. Malcolm growled and pushed Thwart into the Normals, then ran past Zaanan and through a door on the other side of the

room. Three Normals ran after him while two others wrestled Thwart to the floor.

Kara was the head of the Center for Genetic Science, the government agency that determined who should have children and who shouldn't. She had been gathering information on Malcolm for a good while, aware that he had been misusing the Sphere computer to arrange the unrequired matching of people to produce infants that he sold on the black market. The evening before, she had turned her finding into the Judicial Sphere Computer and had been granted permission to arrest Malcolm and hold him for trial.

The two Normals escorted Thwart from the interrogation room. The smoke from the control room burned Kara's eyes. But she walked into the room to wait for the other Normals to return, having no idea that Zaanan was on the table.

"Zaanan!" She could barely believe her eyes. She hadn't been this close to her son since the night he was born. She had seen him from a distance, and even proudly attended his award banquet, but never had any of the pleasure of raising her son, thanks

85

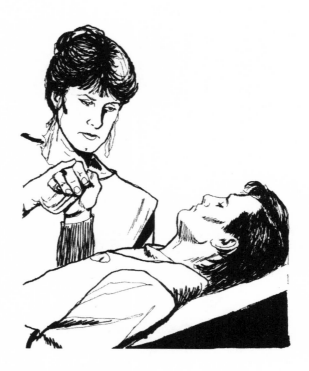

to Sphere's commands of outlawing family life.

Zaanan looked unconscious to her, lying motionless, with his eyes closed. After all these years, she was alone with her son. She stood beside him and studied his face.

"Zaanan," she began, "I am Kara. Your mother."

My mother! Zaanan screamed to himself. The electrical shock still imprisoned his body, but not his mind.

"I know I'm forbidden to speak with you, but if I could, I would say that you have always been in my heart.

Kara unstrapped Zaanan and removed the probe headband. She held his hand as if she wanted something of him to hold onto forever. "You look like your father," she mumbled, fighting back tears she had suppressed since his birth. "I wish there was a way we could all be together, even for a moment."

Zaanan couldn't believe what was happening. Since he was a small boy, he had wanted to be with his mother and father. He wanted to tell her that his father was in the Fatal Limit, and that his brother needed her help, but he couldn't.

86

Kara continued to study his face, etching it into her heart to keep. Tears welled up in Zaanan's eyes. They pooled and then streaked down his cheeks. Kara was shocked to see them. She reached out and brushed them away.

"Zaanan, can you hear me?" she asked as she leaned close to his right ear.

''Malcolm escaped,'' Officer Templer of the Normal police reported.

"We pursued him to the roof, but he escaped in his carcopter. We notified headquarters, and they have alerted the entire department."

The three officers walked into the interrogation room. Kara straightened up and acted as professional and normal as possible. She wanted to take Zaanan with her and be there when the electric shock wore off, but she didn't want to do anything that could hurt his position in the military.

"Take care of Talgent Zaanan and be sure he is taken to his living quarters. He should recover with no ill effects." She marched from the room without looking back even once.

Chapter Eight

A giant screen crackled to life as it received a visual transmission from earth. A gigantic image of Maroth filled the screen. He said nothing for a moment.

The orbiting space colony didn't see him for a moment. An army of people worked feverishly to meet his impossible deadline.

Maroth was the cruel leader of a rebel movement called Troz, the largest group of many that resisted the globalized government of Sphere. This space colony rotated opposite from the moon's rotation, so it would always be on the dark side of the moon. Its purpose was to construct a giant flying robot with virtually indestructible armor.

For weeks the people of Troz had labored in shifts around the clock to complete the robot on schedule. A man named Larkin was the main designer and overseer of the project. He had pleaded with Maroth on numerous occasions to give them more time, but Maroth had refused to change his mind.

Larkin was out in the work area, slaving with all the others, when Maroth's image flashed on the screen. Even though he was bent over tightening a part, he could feel the angry eyes of Maroth behind him. Maroth hadn't spoken, but one by one, the noisy workers silenced.

"Larkin, you have three days. Are you ready?" Maroth's voice bounced off every wall in the colony.
Every worker was already past the point of exhaustion. Larkin was even more stressed, since Maroth's badgering was always aimed at him.

"I hope so," Larkin answered after a long pause.

"You hope so!" growled Maroth.

''Yes, sir. If we had a few more days, even a week, I'm certain we would be ready.''

Every worker stood quietly, hoping for the added workdays. They all felt for Larkin and understood the strain he was under.

"No," said Maroth in an unrelenting manner. "Maroth, it will take us a day to assemble the robot and a day to check it out. We may be able to finish all the parts today, but we can't attack Sphere in three days. I'm sorry. We have done our best, but . . . "

"But nothing," Maroth interrupted. "You are all lazy. I've never had a worker that wasn't lazy. You have no idea how difficult it is leading a people to excellence only to have them pull you down."

Larkin was fed up with Maroth. He heard that same speech every time Maroth spoke.

"If we could just test it somehow, then I would feel more certain of the robot's ability," Larkin petitioned.

There was a long pause before Maroth answered.

"Very well," he agreed. "Take one day to assemble the robot, and then test it by attacking Renaissance, the Sphere Sky prison."

"Renaissance! We can't do that. Blackthorne and a number of our former leaders are in prison there. We must help them, not destroy them!"

The workers murmured among themselves about Maroth's orders. Their voices grew louder in protest.

"Silence!" boomed Maroth. "You will attack Renaissance in thirty-six hours and completely destroy it, or you will all answer to me. I admit that I'm not an easy person, but you have yet to see my bad side."

The visual transmission ended. There was a long pause in the work area as each worker moved toward Larkin, who stood speechless and stunned by Maroth's order.

"What do we do?" Kellner asked.

"Go back to work," Larkin replied, kneeling down to resume work on the part he was adjusting. Slowly each worker followed his lead.

Back on Earth in his remote hideaway, Maroth sat at his desk. He was alone in this fortress. He got up from his black chair and took off his wide-brimmed black hat. Next, he removed his black cowled robe, then pulled off his realistic mask. There stood the evil Maroth, the man of mystery. There stood Malcolm. He began to laugh at his own genius.

All of his life, he had dreamed of being a Talgent warrior for Sphere. He had been reared in the same nursery and school as Zaanan. From childhood they had been the closest of friends and competitors. They went everywhere together. They both chased the dream of being a Talgent. They were equal in their steps toward their goal. With the disappearance of a Talgent named Kassel, an opening was available. Malcolm and Zaanan competed with numerous others for the position. In the end, Zaanan became the Talgent, and Malcolm's friendship turned to utter contempt. Not only did his affection for Zaanan change, but he nursed bitterness toward Sphere, also. He vowed in his heart to one day see Sphere pay for its stupidity.

Malcolm joined the Secret Police and quickly elbowed his way to the top post, then used his position to gain power. He secretly became Maroth and took over the rebel movement called Troz. The robot was his weapon to bring Sphere to its knees. Now he decided he would use the robot to destroy all the former leaders of Troz and Zaanan.

Then he would attack the City of Sphere, as planned. He decided to leak the news to Sphere about the attack on the Renaissance Sky Prison. Malcolm carefully worded the message, so that Sphere would only sense the need to send a Talgent Warrior. A Talgent with power arms could do the job of one hundred soldiers, and Zaanan was Sphere's favorite son.

Chapter Nine

It was early afternoon. Rain pelted on the tall, narrow-paneled windows of Zaanan s living quarters. Zaanan lay in bed, resting. He was no longer stunned, but he did tingle all over. Anytime he tried to move quickly, his muscles would contract painfully.

"Zaanan, Zaanan," called the assignment desk computer from headquarters.

Zaanan carefully got out of bed and walked over to his audio-visual computer. His feet stung as if they had been asleep. There was still a lot of static in his hair.

"Yes? This is Zaanan."

This is a Code R alert. Report to your starjet for further assignment," said the computer.

"Code R," said Zaanan. He forgot all about his discomfort as he dressed in his uniform and donned his lone power arm. He wished he had his other arm that had been damaged by the cavemen down in the volcano. Talgent Flame had promised to have the arm fixed and delivered to him, but she hadn't arrived yet.

Within the hour, Zaanan was flying away from Sphere Space Port in his starjet. Sphere headquarters had already transmitted the mission data to the starjet's on-board computer.

''Report,'' ordered Zaanan as he soared upward.

"Hello, Zaanan," began Calvert Van Hensen's audiovisual message. ''Early this morning we received word that Troz has been secretly building a large military robot. It is called the MFUP, Military Force Unification Project. Details are sketchy, but our source says that it is being tested on our sky prison, Renaissance, tomorrow."

Renaissance, Zaanan thought to himself. That's where Allison and Joseph are being held.

"We haven't been able to communicate with Renaissance, due to a communication malfunction. This warning came so late that we don't have time to move all the prisoners. Your job is to

95

destroy the robot before it reaches the prison."
Zaanan felt a bit uneasy as the message of the Calvert concluded.
There was no information about the size, strength, or vulnerabilities of the robot.

Renaissance was known as a dangerous place. The word
Renaissance means "rebirth." Certain political and ideological
prisoners were kept there, to redirect their thought processes
and allegiance. Many prisoners were as dangerous as they were
brilliant. Zaanan had personally arrested a number of them and
knew how ruthless and cruel they could be. "How long before I
intercept the robot?" Zaanan asked his computer.

"Six hours," the computer replied.

Zaanan set an alarm on his power arm for six hours. "How
long before I reach Renaissance?"

'' At your present speed, you will reach Renaissance in three
hours and thirty minutes," informed the computer.

"I have just over two hours to find and stop the robot. That's
unbelievable," Zaanan complained.

"When you are within range, begin trying to contact Renaissance."

"Yes, sir."

Zaanan's starjet sped on through the lonely barrens of space, toward his most dangerous mission yet.

After two hours of silence, the starjet's computer crackled to life. "You are within range," it reported.

''Good. Try to raise Renaissance on the viewer."

Moments later, a guard was on the screen. "This is Renaissance guard Sullivan speaking."

''Sphere has been trying to reach you for several days now," Zaanan told the man.

"Yes, sir. We've been having some trouble ... with our ... equipment."

"Listen quickly. This is Talgent Zaanan. There's a ... "

"Zaanan!" yelled another voice off-screen. A hand grabbed the guard by the hair on the back of his head and pulled him back. Edolf's face came close to the screen.

"Edolf!" yelled Zaanan.

97

''That's right, Zaanan, '' laughed Edolf. '' Sphere sent me
to this torturous place to 'rebrainwash' me. I thought this place
needed some brainwashing itself, so some old friends of yours
and mine took over. Come see us. It would be like old times.''

"Listen, Edolf. There's a Troz robot on its way to Renaissance
right now to destroy you. My job is to stop it."

"No, Zaanan," Edolf replied, "your job is to come here to Renaissance. Your brother, Joseph, needs to see you. Oh yes, there's
a beautiful young woman with him who needs you, too."

"If you hurt them, I'll see that you regret it forever," Zaanan
threatened.

"Believe me, they are doing fine right now. But they may not
be for long. You have two things we want - you and your starjet.
You come here and surrender, and we'll be sure they make it
back to Earth safely. If you don't, they will meet with a horrible
accident. You have fifteen minutes to get here."

Zaanan had recently arrested Edolf for an attempt to make a
new weapon for the terrorists. His group the Planetarians wanted
to destroy Sphere and dominate the world. For Edolf to lead a

revolt and take over Sphere's maximum-security prison in such a short time proved his leadership ability and criminal genius.

Zaanan knew that Edolf never joked. He was eighteen minutes from Renaissance. Should he ignore Edolf's threat and attack the robot in hopes of sparing the prison? If he did, Edolf would certainly kill Joseph and Allison. Should he surrender to Edolf and ensure Joseph and Allison's safety at the cost of losing Renaissance? Zaanan knew that Allison and Joseph were guilty of alien-thought. They were enemies of his society. The time pad on his instrument panel told him he was at the moment of decision.

He changed his course to arrive at Renaissance in fifteen minutes. From the outside, Renaissance looked as if everything were normal.

"This is Talgent Zaanan. Open up, Edolf, I'm coming in."

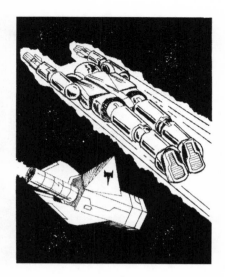

Chapter Ten

A gigantic robot slowly but steadily flew toward the sky prison.

In a spacecraft separate from the robot flew its designer, Larkin, who, along with chief engineer Kellner, continued making last-minute checks.

''All systems are go at this point,'' said Kellner.

''There are a million things that could go wrong, but it does look good,'' admitted Larkin.

"I don't like to think of killing our former leaders," Kellner admitted.

"I don't cherish the idea, either. I wish there was a way to get them out."

"We have a big enough job, keeping this monster together until it's time to attack. Besides, Maroth is our leader now," Kellner reasoned.

"You're right. In a little over an hour, we attack. It's time to wait here and let the robot go on by itself."

Kellner and Larkin hovered in space as the giant robot crept on toward its victims.

Back on Renaissance, Zaanan's starjet made a safe, smooth landing. The landing bay was large, empty, and poorly lighted. Zaanan cautiously disembarked from his vessel.

"Remove your power arm. Let it down and move away from your starjet," Edolf's faceless voice demanded over the intercom system.

Zaanan complied and stepped about twenty paces away from the starjet. A single light beam pierced the dim bay and covered his body. The prison normally used this light beam to escort dangerous criminals from the bay to their cells when they first arrived. Zaanan could only move where the light beam allowed. Edolf walked out of the deep shadows.

"Well, Zaanan, we meet again."

"We have no time to waste. There's a Troz robot on its way

right now to destroy this prison."

"Is this your idea of a trick, Zaanan?"

"Where are Joseph and Allison?" growled Zaanan. He clenched his teeth so hard that his jaw hurt. "They're . . . hanging around. Come along I'll show you."

Zaanan followed Edolf. The light beam restricted his movement somewhat as they walked along a square, barren hallway.

"I suppose I really should be grateful to you," said Edolf. "You spared my life once and sent me here. This place was ripe for rebellion. All they needed was a leader. By the way, do you recall what I was doing down in that volcano?"

"You were foolishly trying to use the volcano heat to form a new destructive alloy. I believe your plan was to make a bomb for terrorism."

"That's correct," Edolf admitted. "But as you know, volcanoes can't be trusted."

Edolf had tried to harness the extreme heat of a volcano to forge a union of magnesium and a new metal called Elementium. This combination, when fused, would have created the deadliest weapon known to man. Edolf was not able to control the volcano

102

as it erupted, but Zaanan's quick thinking had saved Edolf's life.

"Do you know why Sphere created a prison like this?" Edolf asked.

Zaanan didn't answer. Talking seemed to slow Edolf's pace.

"Well, I'll tell you anyway. This is an experimental place, and we are the laboratory rats. For a long time, Sphere gave the sleep injection to anyone who thought differently than it did. However, some 'rats' were considered to be of more value than others. So Renaissance was built as a laboratory for their experiments. Can you imagine my surprise when I arrived here and found out that Sphere was working on the same type of project that I had been? Sphere wanted a weapon to cause the world to finally surrender to it. It's nice to be needed."

"But you needed a volcano to give you enough heat to create your new alloy."

"That's what I thought, too," admitted Edolf. "However, Sphere was one step ahead of me. Let me show you something."

Zaanan was still the prisoner of the light beam as Edolf opened a door in front of them. On the other side, a crowd of inmates had been waiting, like a surprise party. They all cheered as Zaanan and Edolf stepped in.

Many of the faces were familiar to Zaanan. Some he had captured himself. They all laughed to see Zaanan a captive. Edolf led Zaanan into a large, domed room. The crowd parted as they walked by. As the path opened, Zaanan saw Allison and Joseph standing on a small, three-foot platform, tied back-to-back and blindfolded. Steam rose all around them. Zaanan looked down and saw that below them was a giant nuclear reactor. A twofoot-wide catwalk extended twenty-five yards out to the small platform where they were tied.

"Go out to them and set them free. Send them back, and you stay there," ordered Edolf.

"I must have your word that you will take them with you when you leave in my starjet," countered Zaanan.

"Of course, Zaanan. I have no quarrel with them."

104

Released from the light beam, Zaanan started across the cat-walk amid the jeers of the inmates.

"Go back. Save yourself!" Joseph pleaded. Zaanan never broke stride as he reached them. First, he pulled the blindfold off Allison's eyes. She looked up into his strong face. For a brief moment, time stopped as he was hypnotized by her beauty. Neither of them knew what to say. Zaanan, carefully moved around on the swaying platform and untied them. Joseph removed his own blindfold. For the first time in their lives, they met.

"Go on," Zaanan ordered. "A giant robot is about to destroy this place."

Joseph stared at Zaanan for a moment, then walked back across the catwalk with Allison.

''By the way, Zaanan,'' Edolf yelled over, ''I've changed my mind. I've decided to stay and make that weapon. I think I'll attack Sphere."

Everyone roared with laughter as Joseph and Allison arrived safely.

''Good-bye, Zaanan ! '' yelled Edolf as he clicked the device in his hand. The catwalk detached from the platform Zaanan stood on and began slowly retracting. Zaanan's platform hovered

in midair.

"It's time for you to be the next ingredient to sweeten the pot," Edolf laughed.

Allison buried her face in Joseph's arms. She couldn't bear to watch. Edolf clicked the control device, and one side of the platform began to tilt.

Everyone cheered as Zaanan grabbed the top ledge of the platform and held on while the disc continued to tilt over.

Unexpectedly, out of nowhere, someone flew out to Zaanan, grabbed him, and flew across to the other side of the chasm. Talgent Flara! She set him down, dropped his right power arm beside him, and flew back toward Edolf. He was shocked to see her as she fired a stunray at him, just missing him. He dove into the crowd of inmates to escape. Zaanan slipped on his power arm and made the flight across the mouth of the seething reactor. Talgent Flara stood with her back to the door and kept all the inmates from running away.

"Where's Edolf?" Zaanan asked as he landed. "He got away before I could get in position," Talgent Flara replied.

"Do you know where the guards are being held?" Zaanan
asked Joseph.

"Yes. I'll set them free," Joseph said as he and Allison ran past
Flara.

"I'll take care of these guys while you catch Edolf," Talgent
Flara volunteered.

"Thanks, Flame." Zaanan whisked by her and headed for the
bay area where he had landed. He ran down the hallway and into
the bay, to see Edolf trying to open the door of his starjet.

"It's over, Edolf."

Edolf turned and saw Zaanan at the door. He banged his fist
on the starjet door without success, then jumped from the starjet's
wing and picked up Zaanan's discarded power arm.

"Stay back, or I'll slip this on and quake you into space dust,"
he threatened.

Zaanan smiled and continued to walk forward. "I'm warning
you. Stay back!" Edolf screamed. Zaanan walked even closer.

Edolf thrust his hand and arm into the power arm, only to
have an electric shock run up his arm and through his entire

body. He fell to the floor, unconscious. Zaanan bent down and removed the power arm, slipping it on his own arm. That same instant, the alarm went off that Zaanan had set. The giant robot was within firing range.

"Flame, where are you?" Zaanan shouted into his power arm.

''The guards and I have most of the inmates heading back to their cells now.''

"Listen. Get to central control now!"

"I'm on my way."

Zaanan ran as hard as he could to the control room. Once inside, he switched on the outside viewer. About four hundred yards away, the robot waited. Zaanan couldn't believe his eyes. Talgent Flara, Joseph, Allison, and the control room crew dashed into the room with him.

"What is that?" Flara asked.

"Trouble," answered Zaanan. "Do you have anything we can use to defend ourselves?"

"Nothing to defend against something that size," answered the crew chief.

"It's moving," Allison yelled out in warning.

The robot began to vibrate and jerk.

"What are we going to do?" Flara asked.

"I don't know," Zaanan replied.

Joseph, who stood to Zaanan's left, raised his hands, closed his eyes, and prayed out loud. "Father God, in the name of Jesus Christ, I come to You now, asking for a miracle," he prayed. No one bowed a head, but no one tried to stop him. ''The Bible says that no weapon forged against us will prevail. Psalm eighteen, verse two, says, *'The Lord is my rock, my fortress, and my deliverer; my God is my rock, in whom I take refuge. He is my shield and the horn of my salvation, my stronghold.'* Deliver us, and we will give You the glory. Amen."

The room was silent. Suddenly, the robot began breaking into different parts.

"What's happening?" asked Flara.

''It looks like the big robot is made up of hundreds of little aircraft, laser carts, missiles, and other weapons," Zaanan said. The robot completely dismantled into countless pieces of war machinery. For a moment, every piece stopped in space, as if

109

waiting for a signal.

"This is it," Zaanan said slowly.

Allison took Joseph's hand and squeezed it, without looking at him. The trunk of the robot was the only portion that hadn't separated. This was the area in which the land rovers were stored. This trunk began to glow red, and without warning, it blew up, igniting every other part of the disassembled robot. The chain reaction caused the entire robot to explode.

Everyone in central control covered his eyes and jumped for cover. In seconds, the shock wave hit Renaissance and shook it violently. Electrical sparks spewed all over the control room as the power failed. Debris pelted the outer walls of the prison. In moments, the explosion was over and Renaissance's backup system stablized the prison and returned power. They slowly rose to their feet and checked themselves for injuries.

Zaanan walked over to Joseph. "That was some prayer," he said.

"I believe in a great God," Joseph answered.

Zaanan felt awkward. He wanted to hug his brother, but something inside him resisted.

Allison stepped up and took Zaanan's left hand and held it out. Then she took Joseph's right hand and held it out. With her own hands, she held the two brothers' hands together.

Joseph put his left hand on top of Allison's and Zaanan stacked his hand on top of Joseph's. They all laughed as Zaanan reached over and hugged his brother around the neck.

Then he turned to Flara, who stood watching this foreign display of affection. "Flame," he said, "this is my twin brother Joseph."

"You must have family all over the universe," retorted Flara.

Zaanan walked over to her. "I know I have friends. Thank you for the help."

Flara blushed.

"How did you get here, anyway?" Zaanan asked her.

"I told you I'd bring your power arm to you when it was fixed. Actually, Sphere assigned me as your backup."

"I'm really glad of that," Zaanan admitted.

111

Chapter Eleven

Zaanan followed Talgent Flara up into her starjet as she prepared to depart. "Flame," he began awkwardly, "I would appreciate it if you wouldn't say anything about . . . ''

"Your brother?"

"Yes."

"Zaanan, you are the most talented Talgent alive.
You are Sphere's favorite son. You must be careful, or you 're going to get in trouble," she lectured.

"Then you won't tell?"

"Of course ... not," she replied.

Zaanan bent over, kissed her, and left the starjet. "I'm as crazy as he is," Talgent Flara said to herself.

Joseph, Allison, and Zaanan watched as Flara departed.

'' Well, we will go back to our cells now,'' Joseph said.

"No, you're not going to stay here. You weren't sent here legally. I'm taking you back with me.''

Allison and Joseph were ecstatic with joy. Zaanan made sure that Edolf and the other escapees were rounded up, and then they departed.

"We're in for a long trip," Zaanan said as Renaissance faded from view.

"Where are we going?" asked Joseph.

"The Fatal Limit," Zaanan answered.

Joseph smiled and placed his hand on Zaanan's shoulder. Within moments, Allison and Joseph fell asleep, leaving Zaanan alone to pilot the starjet and think. He recalled the words of Asaph. He thought it was so ironic that he gave himself as a ransom for Allison and Joseph. It reminded him of what Asaph had said Jesus did. Gradually that type of love made sense to Zaanan. It was as if his eyes had just been opened. The gospel became

113

clear to him. God really had answered Joseph's prayer about the robot. God really did spare his life as Malcolm was trying to kill him.

God is real, Zaanan thought, as if a light had come on in his head.

He sat motionless for a while as his starjet rocketed across the dark blue velvet night. Tears came to his eyes as he sensed a closeness to the creator of the universe.

"I believe. I believe in Jesus Christ," he said in awe.

. . . To be continued!

114

PRESS

OWL and BOWL Press

TERMS AND PEOPLE YOU WILL READ ABOUT

Alien-thought - Any idea, religion, or movement contrary to Sphere.

Allison - Well-known artist of Sphere.

Asaph - Senior leader of a rebel space colony.

Baron - Military athlete and father of Zaanan.

Edolf - Leader of the terrorist Planetarians.

Fatal Limit - A nuclear waste dump in outer Space. Christians found a way to recycle the waste and use the Limit to power and conceal their Space Colony.

Calvert Van Hensen - Zaanan's superior officer.

Holocaust - Nuclear world war in the twenty-fifth century.

Joseph - Zaanan's twin brother.

Kara - Medical research scientist and mother of Zaanan.

Malcolm - Head of Sphere's Secret Police (SSP).

Maroth - Absolute ruler of Troz.

Normals - Regular Sphere Police Force.

Power arms - Pair of metallic gloves used for protection and communication only by Talgent warriors; powered by nuclear fusion.

Renaissance - A Sphere prison in outer space used for rehabilitation and reprogramming.

Runnlings - A gang of children who banded together after they escaped from Sphere nurseries.

Sleep injection - A shot given that slows down body functions before a person is placed in a frozen state.

Sphere - One-world government of earth ruled by a computer called the Coreum.

Stone, the - A minicomputer that looks like a rock. The computer contains the entire Bible and a concordance. It is activated by forming a fist around it and naming a subject or verse of Scripture. The user's skeleton is used as an amplifier to the user's eardrum.

Talgent Warrior- Highest rank earned by a military specialist

116

who eliminates alien-thought.

Talgent Flara (Flame) - Female Talgent.

Thwart - Malcolm's bumbling assistant.

Troz - The largest of many rebel movements seeking world control over Sphere.

Zaanan - A young military Talgent of the society of Sphere.

ZAANAN
Episode Four: Conflict on Cada-Maylon

Chapter One

Holocaust Year: A.D. 2453
Present Earth Year: A.D. 3007
Year of Sphere: 554
Location: The remote hideaway of Malcolm

"Make every effort to live in peace with all men and to be holy; without holiness no one will see the Lord. See to it that no one misses the grace of God and that no bitter root grows up to cause trouble and defile many." Hebrews 12:14, 15.

All human beings are somehow intertwined together in life. The links in life's chain can be bonds of love or fetters of hate. Both emotions are deeply felt, yet each yields different endings. Stress on love eventually builds character while emphasis on

bitterness leads to corruption and death. Though the boast of bitterness may seem louder than love, it also proves to always be man's weakest link.

Malcolm anxiously paced an imaginary path in the floor of the communication center of his hideaway. The events of his recent past began to filter through his thought processes. He had been the leader of the Sphere Secret Police (SSP): a man of power and position whom others feared. His appetite for more power led him to commit crimes against his own people. When confronted with his misconduct, he fled as a common thief. His purpose in life had been to undermine and overthrow the ruling government of Sphere. He had thoughtfully planned each step he would take to reach his long-range goal of a new world order. He had secretly become the leader of the largest rebel movement named Troz. Disguised as the mysterious Maroth, he used fear and muscle to beat the Trozians into submission. He had also fed enough viral time bombs into the main Sphere computer to eventually weaken

119

its defenses.

Malcolm was particularly uneasy that evening because he was awaiting news that could have been a major step toward his world control. He had lured Talgent Zaanan to Renaissance, Sphere's sky prison. His purpose was two-fold. He would get rid of Zaanan and at the same time destroy the former leaders of Troz imprisoned at Renaissance. He had directed a giant robot to attack the prison and now he marked time hoping for a word of victory.

Alone now with only his thoughts, he took time to rehearse his past. He pulled himself along in his memory, handling each link of bitterness in his life's chain. Each hurtful episode darkened his mood and served to justify his hostility. He was somewhat surprised to recall how many times his life had been coupled with Zaanan's. They had a long history together. He could not recall a time when he didn't know Zaanan. After Malcolm was born, he was immediately taken from his parents and put in a nursery. The

120

Sphere government reared him and programmed him. Malcolm
and Zaanan grew up in the same dormitory and were trained for
military use. Malcolm always viewed himself as short and un-
derweight. His melancholy temperament gave him a bent toward
negative thinking and a low sense of self-worth. He felt things
deeply and was easily provoked. The other boys in his dorm
quickly picked up on his low boiling point. They looked for
every opportunity to make him explode. One day a group of boys
pushed him too far. Oddly enough, Malcolm couldn't recall the
actual deed. Malcolm remembered jumping to his feet and wildly
swinging his fists and feet at a group of jeering boys. He firmly
connected with several punches, which changed their laughter to
anger. The entire group of boys began beating and kicking him.
All these years later the sting of their blows still seemed just as
painful and real. Seemingly out of nowhere, Zaanan dove into
the small riot. In seconds everyone knew that Zaanan was on
Malcolm's side. The fight was fierce, but in the end Malcolm and
Zaanan stood back to back breathing heavily. Slowly they

circled, daring any attackers to come near. The boys backed away and dispersed. Malcolm turned toward Zaanan. The emotion of the moment welled up in Malcolm's throat. He couldn't allow himself to cry in front of his peer, so he ran. He bolted out of the dormitory and sprinted as fast and far as he could. His side ached until he finally fell to the ground. Dirt mixed with his tears as his body convulsed in wave after wave of sorrow. He hated Sphere. He hated his parents. He hated those boys who made fun of him. He hated authority. Most of all he hated himself. He vowed to himself to never let anyone make him cry again. He would never be conquered or surpassed by anyone or anything. He cried deeply until he fell asleep. When he awoke night had fallen and the moon was full. The grass around him was wet with dew. He was tired and emotionally drained as he turned over and sat up. There seated a few yards away was Zaanan. Malcolm pulled himself to his feet and began the journey back to the dormitory. Zaanan fell in beside him. Neither spoke a word going back.

Long ago Malcolm's memory had suppressed that day. For a moment Malcolm remembered the love and admiration he had for his friend Zaanan. Love had linked them together as friends and they were as close as brothers. They went everywhere together and competed against each other in everything. Each test of life seemed to come effortlessly to Zaanan, while everything was a struggle for Malcolm. His determination and Zaanan's talent seemed to always put them neck and neck in any race or test. Zaanan seemed to spend much of his time encouraging the somber Malcolm. It was true that Malcolm had a healthy love for Zaanan, but he also always viewed Zaanan as his ultimate foe. He could conquer the world, but if he wasn't better than Zaanan he would consider himself a failure.

"Maroth, sir! ... this is Larkin," said a voice piercing the silence of Malcolm's mental trip. For a few seconds Malcolm didn't respond.

"Please come in, sir," requested Larkin. Malcolm aroused as if out of a trance. He grabbed his Maroth costume and put it on.

"You have good news I hope," said Maroth as he came on

Larkin's viewer screen. Larkin, Maroth's chief engineer, and his assistant Kellner sat motionless for a brief moment.

"Report," ordered Maroth. His voice was synthetically altered to enhance his disguise and conceal his true identity.
Larkin and Kellner sat mute in their space craft, squirming about in their chairs trying to get comfortable.

"Well, answer me!" screamed Malcolm with such force that his words almost echoed.

"The robot . . . ex . . . exploded as . . . "

"What!" thundered Maroth in a voice so angry, so loud, that both Larkin and Kellner literally jumped.

"Yes, yes sir ... it ex-exploded," replied Larkin as if the word "explode" was the most difficult of words to speak. Maroth sat quietly seething.

"All systems were go on the robot. It was dismantling into its different weapons when it suddenly exploded," Larkin continued.

124

"And Renaissance?" asked Maroth.

"The prison . . . was . . . unharmed," answered Kellner as he shifted in his seat. He looked away to break eye contact with Maroth. Maroth's stern silence was just as loud as his yell. Maroth was severely disappointed. His hopes of eliminating Zaanan and the former Trozian leaders were dashed.

A victory at Renaissance would have built more faith in his leadership among the people of Troz. He needed their loyalty to reach his ultimate goal of ruling over Sphere and the world. Malcolm had spent a lot of time and energy building power, mystery and fear into the Maroth character. Until this defeat he had appeared almost supernatural to them.

As Maroth sat in silence, fear mounted in Larkin and Kellner. With one word he could sentence them to reprogramming or death.

Suddenly, Maroth changed his disposition.

"That will be all," stated Maroth minus any anger in his voice. Transmission ceased.

Larkin and Kellner sat staring at the blank visual screen for a

moment and slowly looked at each other.

"What do we do?" asked Kellner.

"I don't know," replied Larkin after a moment. " I guess we should return to the space colony."

"Are ... are we going to die for this?" wondered Kellner. Larkin sat silently for a long moment, then he hit the flight controls. The space craft began to move toward their base.

Back at Maroth's hideout he, too, stared at the blank screen. Once again Zaanan had eluded him.

"We will meet again, Zaanan," said Malcolm out loud as if Zaanan were standing in front of him. "We will meet again."

Chapter Two

Jameston stood before a large glass window. He came every night to the same spot and remained for at least an hour. He spent as many of his daytime hours as possible on the other side of that very window. It was the view window for the newborn infant nursery. Jameston was deep in thought as he argued with himself about his evil mission. That night seemed to be a time of reflection for many people.

Jameston had been reared in a Sphere nursery, vastly different from this nursery. He was separated at birth from his parents and owned by the Sphere government. The infants before him would

be united with their parents in a day or two. Jameston had lived
his sixty-two years under Sphere's watchful eye. He had been
somewhat content with his two jobs. At age fifty-five he was
given the life extension test and passed. Each year the test became more difficult, yet he passed. However, on his sixty-second
birthday he failed the exam. He searched his mind trying to recall
where he had messed up, but couldn't. People who failed the test
were given the sleep injection and eventually frozen. After thirty
years they were discarded.

Malcolm, the leader of the SSP, stepped in and spared him.
Malcolm said he would grant Jameston a permanent life extension in exchange for information. Infants and the elderly of
Sphere were disappearing at an alarming rate. Jameston was
to somehow join those kidnapped and report back to Malcolm.
Jameston left the testing center. In the dead of night, he was
contacted by two masked men who invited him to escape with

them to safety. He eagerly consented and was brought to the Fatal Limit. He was more than willing to help Malcolm uncover the kidnappers until he saw the babies. Children were always kept separate from adults, so Jameston had never seen an infant. Now he was torn between his promise to Malcolm and his feelings about his newfound home.

The Fatal Limit was universally known as a nuclear radiation and toxic waste dumping territory in space. A band of Christians had to escape the Sphere government because their beliefs were contrary to the Sphere philosophy. They found a way to convert the deadly poisons of the Limit into safe power. They built a space colony in the middle of the Limit and used the dangerous radiation as a protective shield. Part of the believers' mission was to rescue undesired·infants and old people.

"I know how you feel," said a voice behind Jameston. Jameston was startled by his company. He whirled around and there stood Asaph, the senior pastor of the Christians.

129

"I never grow tired of the miracle of new life," said Asaph
as he glided his air-walker up to the window next to Jameston.
Jameston didn't speak; he just turned toward the window and
continued looking.

"I never grow weary of seeing humans born or born-again,"
mused Asaph, again breaking the silence. Jameston didn't understand what Asaph said, but he nodded his head in agreement.

"My name is Asaph," he volunteered, "and you're?"

"Jameston, from the city of Sphere."

"It's nice to meet you," stated Asaph. "I watched you today
from this very spot. There seems to be a special bond between
you and the little dear ones."

"I don't know'. Maybe it's that I've never seen babies before."

"Asaph," interrupted a voice over the intercom system.

"Yes."

"Zaanan, Allison and Joseph are landing in Bay number 2 right now," informed the voice.

"Joseph!" glistened Asaph, "I'm on my way right now. It was nice meeting you, Jameston, I hope we can spend more time together later. We're very happy you are with us."

Asaph turned his air-walker toward the bay area. Jameston turned back toward the big window and continued his mental wrestling match.

"I can't wait to see Asaph," said Zaanan as he helped Allison disembark from his starjet.

"I can't wait to see him either," said Joseph as he joined them on the deck of the arrival bay.
In moments Asaph met them in the hallway on level two of the space station. Joseph ran to greet him. They embraced.

"My prayers have been answered today as never before," sobbed Asaph as he hugged his Joseph. He had reared Joseph from the time he was born and always viewed him as a son. Zaanan noticed the affection they had for each other.

Though Joseph was Zaanan's twin brother, they were brought up very differently. As a citizen of Sphere, Zaanan had been parented by the cold, sterile government. Zaanan realized what he had missed as he witnessed the glad reunion. Allison picked up on Zaanan's response and put her hand on Zaanan's arm and gently squeezed.

"Zaanan, Allison, come near," invited Asaph. He hugged them both. "Now more than ever I believe in miracles. I feared I'd never see any of you alive again. Come, tell me everything that happened."

"How is my father?" asked Zaanan.

"We have been diligently working on your father, but we haven't actually tried to awaken him."

Zaanan's father had failed the life-extension test in Sphere. He was given the sleep injection but hadn't been frozen. Zaanan brought his father to Asaph in hopes that the Christians might have the technology to awaken him.

132

Over the next hour or so all three young people took turns telling their version of their recent adventures. When everyone seemed to have run out of story, Zaanan decided it was time to tell his special news.

"Asaph, do you remember your final words to me before I left here last time?"

"I believe I said that I'd be praying for you," answered Asaph.

"Your actual words were that you'd be praying that I would see the reality of God in this situation. Well, when Malcolm had me strapped to a table and about to kill me, I prayed. Malcolm had stunned me with a stun-gun. My body was helpless, but my mind was completely awake. I prayed if there was a God, He'd do something to spare me!" Zaanan said as he acted out the scenario. "Suddenly, from nowhere the Normal police broke into the control room. They had come to arrest Malcolm for some kind of crime. Malcolm escaped, but to my surprise the leader of the arrest team turned out to be Kara, our mother!"

Everyone sat speechless for a moment.

"What did she say - what did you say?" asked Joseph.

"I couldn't say anything, I couldn't even open my eyes. She whispered that I had always been in her heart and that she wished we could all be together as a family."

Asaph, Allison and Joseph all sat still, encouraging Zaanan to continue.

"When Joseph prayed at Renaissance and the robot exploded, I was in awe," said Zaanan. "As we journeyed here I had time to think about everything that has happened to me in these last few weeks. I realized that all this had a purpose. God really is real. Anyway, as we were on our way here I - I committed my life to Jesus Christ."

Everyone sat quietly stunned by Zaanan's announcement. He blinked hard and felt awkward and somewhat bewildered. All at once Joseph and Allison jumped to their feet and hugged Zaanan.

"The angels in heaven are rejoicing just as we are!" said Asaph through tears of joy.

"I'm a little confused about what to do now," said Zaanan.

"Don't worry, my boy, we will help you. First we must enroll you in our discipleship course and ... " suggested Asaph.

"I'm afraid I can't stay too long," said Zaanan, "I've got to return to Sphere."

''Then we will give you a crash course of basic beliefs," said Asaph.

This pleased Zaanan and he was eager to begin. After a good meal and some rest, Zaanan reported to the educational section of the space colony. Over the next few days, he attended classes and share groups where he learned basic doctrines, ordinances and Christian history. He was taught how to study the Stone, a minicomputer that contained the entire Holy Bible and a full concordance. A fist would be made around it and the user's skeleton

135

would be used as an amplifier to the eardrum. The Stone was the Christians' most prized secret because Sphere outlawed any books or beliefs different from Sphere's philosophy.

History was actually Zaanan's favorite seminar. It was taught in a circular room with a large lighted stage in the center. Bleacher-like seats filled up the remainder of the room. Lifesize holograms of actors enacted the stories of the Old and New Testaments. Should a scene require more room, such as depicting a city or something at sea, the players and props would simply shrink to a proportional size. Zaanan was fascinated by everything he heard. His hunger to know God and about God was ravenous. Each moment God became more real to him. At mealtime all he could speak of was what he had learned that day. He couldn't understand anyone not wanting to experience Jesus Christ. Asaph, Joseph and Allison laughed with joy as Zaanan shared each concept as if none of them had ever heard it before.

136

Those were indeed happy days for Zaanan. He was beginning
to feel as if he would never leave the Fatal Limit. Every spare
moment he had he spent praying, studying, or sitting by Baron,
his father. Baron was the only flicker in Zaanan's steady flame.
It seemed that the doctors weren't any closer to reviving Baron
from his sleep. Hour by hour Baron lay peacefully slumbering in
his sleep tube. He slowly rotated on a cushion of fog or smoke
that partially concealed his body. Everyone readily noticed the
change in Zaanan, including Allison. She seemed to take great
interest in his newfound faith and also in him as a man. Joseph
teased Zaanan and referred to him fondly as "Zaanan the Zealot."

One evening most of the colony residents had gone to sleep.
Zaanan was still up trying to study but with little success. His
eyelids felt as if they weighed tons. He nodded off to sleep resting his chin on his folded arms.

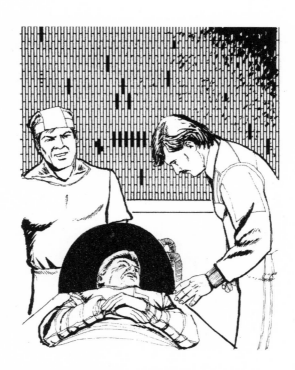

"Zaanan," blared a voice over the intercom in his room. He jumped and tried to awaken.

"Yes, I'm here."

"Please hurry to the medical center," requested the faceless voice. Zaanan knew it had something to do with his father, so he ran as fast as he could. As he arrived he was greeted by Asaph, Joseph and a small group of doctors.

''They've given him medication that should reverse the effects of the sleep injection."

Seconds seemed like years as they carefully watched Baron for any kind of movement. Zaanan got down on his knees close to the sleep tube. He studied Baron's body for a sign.

"He moved his hand!" yelled Zaanan. "I saw him move his hand!"

Everyone looked more closely. Baron's eyelids fluttered and he groaned a sigh.

"He's awake!" said Joseph.

The doctors carefully lifted the lid on the sleep tube and

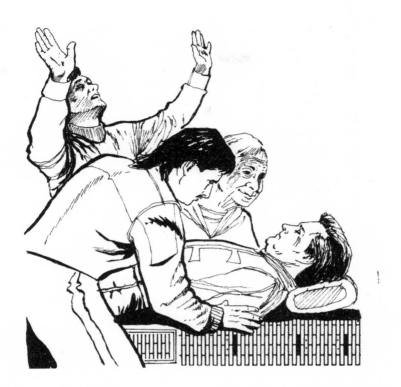

placed an oxygen mask over his nose and mouth. Their instruments indicated that he was waking up. The doctors quickly covered his chest, neck, and head with vital sign monitors. Slowly but progressively, he continued to arouse. He opened his eyes and looked around. He squinted from the bright lights.

"Father!" Zaanan exclaimed as he leaned over his father. Baron didn't seem to respond to his voice.

"Give him a minute, my son," admonished Asaph. "He's been asleep for a good while."

"Thank you, Jesus," said Zaanan with tears streaming down his face. He raised his hands toward heaven as if desiring to reach God and hug Him. Joseph stood on the left side of his father and anxiously waited.

"Can you believe we're a family again?" said Zaanan to Joseph.

Joseph tried to answer, but the lump in his throat was too large. He just smiled and returned to watching his father. Zaanan

139

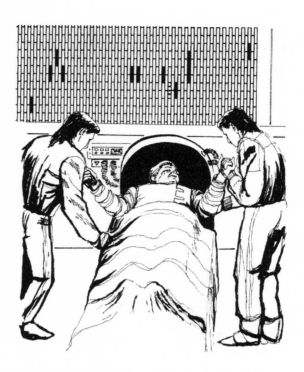

suddenly realized he was crying. This emotion was so foreign to his personality that he marveled at the release he felt.

"Where - am - I?" mumbled Baron haltingly. His face was still somewhat numb.

"You are among friends," answered Asaph, leaning over Baron.

Baron's eyes began to focus somewhat on Asaph.

"As - Asaph?" said Baron, short of breath.

"He is waking up!" squealed Asaph. Zaanan and Joseph rushed to his side.

''Baron, allow me to introduce you to your two sons, Talgent Zaanan and Joseph.''

Both boys grabbed a hand and squeezed it.

Baron drowsily looked at both boys and smiled. Joseph and Zaanan looked at each other. That moment their lives were relinked by love.

"You'd better let him rest now," advised a doctor. ''Come back in the morning.''

Reluctantly the boys released their father's hands. They came around at the foot of the sleep tube and embraced. It was a beautiful moment in their lives.

"I only wish our mother was here," said Joseph.

"That's my next personal mission," said Zaanan happily.

As they walked out of their father's room, an alarm went off above their heads. They turned around to see doctors rush to their father's side.

"Baron!" yelled Zaanan.

Everything seemed to go into slow motion as the brothers flew to his side.

"Please step back," asked a doctor impatiently as he nudged past Zaanan and Joseph.

"Baron!" yelled Zaanan again.

"We're losing him," said a doctor as he attempted to administer treatment.

"Get them out of here!" ordered the doctor again.

Five orderlies came in and attempted to remove the brothers.

Zaanan resisted their overtures, so they grabbed him and began to pull him out. Zaanan's temper flared hot as they physically removed him. He was about to resort to fighting when his eyes fell on Asaph. Asaph's face was sober and gray. He never uttered a word, but his wrinkled glance stopped Zaanan in his tracks.

"You can't do any good here," said Asaph. "The doctors will do what's best."

Zaanan knew this in his mind, but his heart didn't want to chance losing his father again. He stumbled into the hallway. His knees were shaking and he felt sick at his stomach. He slumped to the floor. Joseph slipped down beside him. Joseph quietly prayed to himself. Zaanan saw his lips moving. Zaanan felt no faith, no power. He knew he should pray, but the hurt was too deep. Zaanan sat there for what seemed to be an eternity. Actually only twenty minutes passed before Asaph glided his air-walker into the hallway.

"Your father is alive," said Asaph plainly.

142

Zaanan looked up at Asaph and felt ashamed of his outburst.

"I'm sorry for the way I acted," apologized Zaanan.

"I believe you behaved normally under the circumstances. I probably would have done the same," reassured Asaph.

"Will he be all right?" asked Joseph as he broke his long silence.

"Well," began Asaph, "the doctors feel that his blood pressure increased too quickly, which caused a severe stroke. One side of his body is paralyzed, and he can't speak."

"Will he stay like that?" asked Joseph.

"No one really knows that. In time he may bounce back," answered Asaph. "However, he may have another stroke. We've never revived anyone from the sleep injection before we . . . "

"Sphere," retorted Zaanan angrily. His blood began to boil.

"Sphere?" quizzed Asaph.

"I'm sick of Sphere playing god! What gives it the right to decide who lives or dies? I'll pay Sphere back if it's the last thing I do" barked Zaanan as he rose to his feet.

"Revenge is God's business and His alone," reminded Asaph as he interrupted Zaanan.

A loud alarm went off that awakened the entire space colony. Red lights flashed a general alarm up and down each corridor.

"What's wrong?" asked Joseph.

Asaph pressed a button on his air-walker.

''What is it?" asked Asaph of Colony Control.

"Someone has barricaded himself in the communications area and is trying to signal Sphere," informed a voice from Colony Control.

"I'm on my way," said Asaph.

Joseph and Zaanan jumped to their feet. In a flash they were down the hallway and down three levels to the Colony Control Deck. A small crowd had formed outside the door of the

144

communication center. Zaanan bobbed over the heads of the
crowd to get a look at the intruder through a thick window beside
the door.

"Who is he? Does anyone know him?" asked Zaanan of anyone there.

"He's new," said someone in the group.

"His name is James - something," answered another.

Inside the Communications Center two sweaty hands choked
a microphone holder. Perspiration poured down Jameston's face
as he frantically tried to reach Sphere with a message.

"Malcolm . . . come in Malcolm," repeated Jameston over and
over. "This is Jameston; please answer me."

"Everyone stand back, I'm going to break the glass," said
Zaanan. Zaanan found a steel bar to hit the large thick window.

"Wait, he has a laser gun!" warned Joseph. "If you break in
there and he fires that gun it could blast a hole through to the surface. In seconds the entire colony could be contaminated."

"We must stop him before he reaches Sphere," blared Zaanan.
"Is there any other way intos the room?"

"Yes, there is. On the other side of the center. He may have
forgotten about the other entrance."

Just then through the glass everyone saw Asaph glide into
view. Zaanan climbed over people to get next to the glass window. He could only guess what was going on inside since he
couldn't hear through the glass. Jameston, who was startled by
Asaph's presence, turned and pointed the laser gun at him. Asaph
didn't move any closer. His face was almost angelic in appear-
ance. Jameston removed the microphone from its holder and
positioned himself to call Malcolm and watch Asaph at the same
time. Zaanan strained to read their lips but failed. The crowd in
the hall grew.

"We've got to stop that man, Joseph," yelled Zaanan into the
crowd. He couldn't see his brother anywhere. Zaanan turned and
faced the crowd as the people pressed against him trying to see

146

what was happening. In the back he saw Joseph motioning him to
hurry. Zaanan began the near impossible task of getting out.

"We've got to get in there!" screamed Zaanan above the
crowd's noise.

"Come with me!" yelled Joseph in reply. Once again, they
hurriedly knifed their way through the ever-growing throng of
people.

Inside Asaph was cool and reassuring, but Jameston was wild-
eyed, frightened, and nearly delirious.

"Malcolm ... said he'd kill me if I didn't tell where you are,"
blubbered Jameston. "I don't want to hurt my babies."

"Jameston, put down the gun. I won't let Malcolm hurt you or
your babies."

"I don't want to hurt my babies," cried Jameston.

"Give me the gun and I'll take you to your babies," said
Asaph.

"I'm so tired," said Jameston.

147

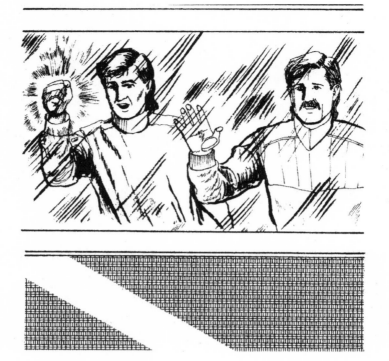

Joseph and Zaanan elbowed their way free from the crowd and began a long run to reach the other side of the Communications Center. They ran as hard as they could.

"I'm just so tired," said Jameston.

It was apparent to Asaph that Jameston was weakening. He glided a little closer. Jameston seemed to revive a little and raised the gun. "You don't want to harm me, Jameston," said Asaph. Zaanan finally reached the door. It was locked.

"It won't open!" said Zaanan.

"It must be locked from the inside."

"Open up!" screamed Zaanan as he pounded on the door. He then began throwing his weight against the door, trying to burst it open. They looked in the thick window next to this new door. They banged on the window, trying to get Asaph to open the door. Once again in pantomime they watched Asaph trying to get the gun away from Jameston who appeared very weak. Finally Jameston sat listless. Apparently, Asaph asked for the gun

148

again because he held it out. Before Asaph could reach it, the gun dropped and discharged.

Ka-Boom!

The laser cut right through the ceiling and the outside shell of the Colony. Zaanan and Joseph covered their eyes for a second because of the brilliance of the explosion. Gases, vapors, and smoke flooded the Communication Center. Asaph and Jameston both grabbed their throats and fell to the floor.

"No! No! No!," shouted Zaanan angrily as he pounded on the window.

Almost in seconds trained emergency personnel arrived and sealed off the area. Dressed in protective clothing, they closed off the area. They had to get inside to Asaph without spreading the radiation. In a matter of moments, they cut their way inside with torches that used extreme low temperatures to freeze-cut the door. Zaanan watched as they picked up both men and put them into inflated envelopes that stretched the length of their bodies.

One part of the crew began to patch the hole to the outside while the others worked on getting Asaph and Jameston out to safety.

Zaanan and Joseph hurried as fast as they could back to the Medical Center. They arrived just as the door closed on the emergency team, Asaph, and Jameston. An electronic sign flashed the words ''Danger-Radiation'' on the face of the door. Zaanan and Joseph wanted to break down the door but they knew it would be foolish. After they waited for an hour, they decided to go back to their rooms to rest and wait.

Chapter Three

The remainder of the night cycle in the Space Colony seemed longer than the actual few hours it was. Zaanan tried to sleep but couldn't. He felt as if he had been tripped and beaten. Zaanan gave up on the idea of sleep, so he just lay there as his mind raced a thousand different confused directions. Zaanan heard a light knock on his door.

"Enter," said Zaanan as he sat up in bed. He hadn't bothered to remove his now wrinkled clothing.

"I'm sorry about last night," said Allison as she entered his small room. Zaanan said nothing at first. He got up and pressed a button on a panel beside his bed. A small water sink extended out

from the wall about eighteen inches. He splashed cold water on his face and blotted it dry with a towel.

"I feel - numb today," said Zaanan. "I don't feel happy or sad, just numb."

''You are feeling normal considering what happened and your lack of rest."

"No, I'm afraid it's deeper than that. Yesterday I felt great. God was so near to me and life couldn't get any better. Then, for no apparent reason it's all gone. It's almost like God saw that I was having such a wonderful time and He decided to cut me down," reasoned Zaanan. "I'm angry at God and that makes me feel confused. Where was God when all this was going on? Why didn't He stop it? If He knows everything, where was He?" Allison listened quietly as Zaanan's mood darkened. She wanted to say just the right words to comfort him but couldn't think of anything.

"I thought the Stone told us how God is supposed to act and how we're supposed to act," flashed Zaanan as he circled the room.

152

"God will not climb into your little box. He's not a formula that you can deal with mathematically," answered Allison. "The Stone not only teaches us how to act but how to react to life. The scriptures aren't only written to raise your level of education but to actually feed your spirit. Zaanan, God's ways are above our ways. In time all this will make sense, I promise you."

Zaanan walked over and faced the wall. He rested his forehead against the wall. Allison walked up behind him and leaned against his back.

"In a way, I'm glad this happened now," said Allison.

"Glad?" replied Zaanan.

"Eventually you were going to have to begin to face the trials of your faith. None of us will escape being tested. You'll learn that prosperity and poverty are both tests. The Stone says in the book of James chapter one and verse two through four: 'Consider it pure joy, my brothers, whenever you face trials of many kinds, because you know that the testing of your faith develops perseverance. Perseverance must finish its work so that you may be

153

mature and complete not lacking anything!' "

Allison couldn't sense his defenses change at all.

"In the book of first Peter it says that your faith is like refined gold. When gold is first mined it is full of impurities. At the refinery the gold is placed in fire. At various temperatures different impurities are burned off, eventually leaving pure gold. Zaanan, bad things happen in life to everyone. Don't run from God now. Allow God to use this to purify you and you will come out stronger. Decide now to live by verses five and six of Proverbs chapter three: *'Trust in the Lord with all your heart and lean not on your own understanding; in all your ways acknowledge him, and he will make your paths straight.'* "

Allison walked to the door. Zaanan turned to look at her.

"The kingdom of this world is based on your abilities and strength. The Kingdom of God is based on your availability to Him and His strength in you," concluded Allison as she walked from the room.

He bathed and then went to the Medical Center. Joseph was

154

already there. Asaph and Jameston were encased in large plastic transparent tents. The medical staff attended to their needs using robotic arms. Both men looked terribly ill and weak. Monitors and tubes reflecting the latest in medical technology covered their bodies. Zaanan walked up close and pressed his hands gently on the tent.

"Asaph, I'm sorry this happened," said Zaanan. Asaph didn't respond.

"It's time I go back to Sphere," said Zaanan.

He turned and walked out of the room. In his room he collected his things and headed for his starjet. He opened the cockpit to get in, but Joseph was seated in his seat.

"Going anywhere?" asked Joseph.

"I was about to ask you the same question," said Zaanan as he dumped his belongings inside. "I'm staying, I'm needed here for a while. Why are you leaving?"

"It's time I go," said Zaanan without looking at Joseph.

"Why?"

155

"Listen," flared Zaanan, "I could not make out everything that crazy man said last night through the glass, but I did pick up three words, "Come in Malcolm!""

"So, you're going after Malcolm," reasoned Joseph.

"Yes, and you aren't going to stop me!"

"I wouldn't try," said Joseph.

"Malcolm imprisoned Allison, sent you both to Renaissance, and caused that crazy man to harm Asaph. I wouldn't be surprised if he had our father given the injection."

"He has done a lot wrong, hasn't he? But it reminds me of the story in the book of Matthew, chapter eighteen.

"You Christians never miss a chance to throw rocks, do you?" retorted Zaanan. "You have a story for everything."

Joseph got up from Zaanan's seat and let Zaanan sit down. The Talgent hastily made ready for his departure.

"I went by your room before I came here. I noticed that you forgot something."

Joseph held out the Stone that Asaph had once given Zaanan. Zaanan didn't reach out to take it, so Joseph dropped it in his lap. Zaanan's starjet roared to life as he slipped on his power arms.

156

Joseph stood back as Zaanan blasted off for earth. Zaanan followed the links of bitterness on his own life's chain because he knew they would eventually lead him to Malcolm.

Chapter Four

As Zaanan's starjet streaked through space, his mood darkened just as dark as the space around him. Hurt had taken over reason in his heart. All he could think about was how for the first time in his life he opened up his mind to love only to be disappointed. He didn't want to think about God or anything except killing Malcolm.

In the course of time Zaanan was entering earth's aerospace. He contacted Sphere and was granted landing permission.

''Star jet 134-J, you are cleared for landing in Bay 6-B.'' said Space Port Control. "Supreme Calvert Van Hensen orders you to

headquarters for immediate assignment."

"Acknowledged," answered an emotionless Zaanan.

Thirty minutes later Zaanan was on his way to headquarters. As he walked the street everything seemed different. His attitude toward Sphere and life in general had changed. His outlook had soured as if something was eating at his insides.
He made his way into the building and to the Calvert's office suite.

"Zaanan!" said the Calvert as he cheerfully greeted his comrade. "It's wonderful to see you again."

Zaanan took a seat in front of the Calvert's large desk.

The Calvert was kind, but he rearranged objects around his desk as if out of nervous habit.

"Nice job, saving Renaissance and all," said the Calvert, looking up from his desk.

"Thank you, sir."

159

The Calvert rose from his seat, went to his window and looked out. A giant live action billboard was directly across the street. Through his window a large eye, nose and mouth could be seen of a woman advertising "Glint," the new soft drink from the pleasure division of Sphere.

"As you know, Malcolm is now a fugitive of Sphere. I never had a good feeling about him," said the Calvert without looking at Zaanan. "We've gone through his home, office, everything, looking for clues to his whereabouts. His files uncovered an unbelievable amount of criminal activity. Do you realize . . . '' said Van Hensen; then he caught himself. "Don't get me started."

Zaanan remained silent, listening to everything his superior said.

"Even his assistant Thwart has dropped from view," continued Van Hensen.

"Calvert Van Hensen, I request permission to speak," said an

information officer over the Calvert's viewer screen.

"Permission granted."

''We have a source who claims to have spotted Malcolm in the St. Gotthard Mountains of old Europa. He was last seen in a village near our Europa Retreat Center III."

"I'm on my way," said Zaanan shooting out of his seat.

"Have all data transmitted to Zaanan's starjet and me," ordered Van Hensen.

"Yes sir," said the information officer as he signed off.

In no time Zaanan was on his way to Europa. During the flight Zaanan carefully reviewed all the information stored in his onboard computer. Zaanan had never been to Europa before. Europa was the German pronunciation for what once was Europe. The Germans had been the last to dominate all the European states before the nuclear Holocaust of 2453 A.D. His instruments indicated that he was flying over the Maritime Alps of what once

161

was France. He turned northeastward toward the base of St. Gotthard Pass. Within minutes Zaanan landed his craft and reported to the small military main office. He was always amazed how local styles of construction were meshed with Sphere architecture.

Weather patterns had become unpredictable since the Holocaust. In this portion of the world a huge cold air mass had settled, causing an unusually long winter.

Zaanan sat on a small chair in the office foyer. Apparently, there was little heat in the building because everyone he saw still had on their heavy coats. The office area was cluttered and dusty. He could tell that this resort area definitely wasn't on the fighting edge in the war on alien-thought. The atmosphere was cold but relaxed in comparison with the City of Sphere.

"Ah - Talgent Zaanan," said a tall, thin, balding man as he walked from his office. "I've heard so much about you. It's a pleasure to have you in our little hamlet."

162

Zaanan stood but said nothing.

"Would you care for some Kaffee (coffee)?" he asked politely.

"No, where is Malcolm?" asked Zaanan bluntly.

The man smiled and rubbed his hands together to warm them.

"Living here I forget the urgent manner of people from the City of Sphere. I don't know, maybe it's the quietness of snow that tends to make us reposed."

Zaanan walked to the door and opened it. A gust of wind blew a flurry of snow into the office. "If you are coming with me, get your hat," ordered Zaanan.

The officer hurried to his office and emerged positioning his fur cap on his head. He walked past Zaanan, who closed the door behind himself. The officer now behaved in a more official manner. They tramped through the powder to a group of Pep-Skids. A Pep-Skid was a thin, powered ski with a handle much

163

like a scooter. The operator turned the ski by dragging one foot
on the side of the ski to which he wished to turn. Zaanan wasn't
familiar at all with the Pep-Skid. The officer got on his and took
off. Zaanan watched him and tried to emulate the officer. He got
it started and everything seemed fine until it came time to turn.
It required practice to learn how much turning friction was required. He put his left foot down but not enough. His Pep-Skid
didn't turn. He leaned his body weight and lost control. He pulled
back on the throttle and the Pep-Skid jumped to hyperspeed. People who leisurely strolled the village streets began to run for their
lives to keep from getting skidded. Zaanan cleared a path forty
yards long. Directly in front of him was a six-foot snow drift on
the side of a watch shop.

"Ka-Plow!"

Zaanan hit the drift with his head-first and was left with only his
feet showing. A crowd gathered around. Two men grabbed his

feet and pulled him out. Everyone cheered, clapped, and laughed as Zaanan lay there on his stomach. He hoped they would all go away before he turned over. Someone walked up next to him. Zaanan could tell from the toes of his boots it was the officer. Zaanan looked up. The officer looked like his head reached the sky.

"Well, was Malcolm in the snow bank?" asked the officer curtly.

Zaanan stood to his feet and brushed the snow from his hat and clothing. The officer didn't offer to help as he stood motion-less waiting for an answer.

"No - he wasn't," said Zaanan now deflated. The crowd cheered and laughed again. Zaanan sheepishly scanned the faces of the gathering. There in the crowd stood . . . .

"Malcolm!" yelled Zaanan.

Malcolm turned and ran.

Zaanan jumped into the crowd. People were joyous about the freak accident. They were all patting Zaanan on the back and

treating him as a mock hero. As Zaanan finally broke free of the
people, he saw Malcolm run around a corner about twenty yards
away.

"He's headed for the Snowrail station!" yelled the officer as he
caught up to Zaanan. He stopped and blew a whistle to alert the
Normal police of trouble.

Europa Retreat Center III was one of many Sphere resorts
throughout the world. When a man and woman were selected
to reproduce, they were sent to a resort to be together until the
female became pregnant. While there the people could enjoy any
of the sports activities the resort area provided. The Snowrail was
a monorail train that carried sightseers and skiers through the St.
Gotthard Pass to their ski lifts.

Skiers were waiting in line to give their boarding passes to a
conductor. Malcolm looked back and saw Zaanan in hot pursuit.
Malcolm picked up his stride and jumped in front of the last two
boarders.

''You haven't got a pass!'' objected the conductor. Malcolm turned around, grabbed the pass from the man behind him and pushed him down. Malcolm plopped the pass on the conductor's chest and pushed him aside. Then he jumped aboard and began elbowing his way to the front of the train. In that instant the train began to move out of the station.

Zaanan, the officer, and a group of Normals stopped at the station platform and watched the Snowrail pick up speed.

"We missed him," said the officer.

"Maybe you did," answered Zaanan. He threw off his heavy jacket and exposed his power arms.

"Flight Mode," he yelled. Zaanan flew toward the train. Power arms could only propel him so far before he had to leap again. He was airborne for a quarter mile, landed, and then jumped back into the air. This time he caught up with the Snowrail, which had to slow down for a curve. He grabbed on to the top of the train at the joint between the third and fourth cars. The metal surface was

cold and slippery, especially at the incline the train was climbing. He pulled himself up and stood to his knees. The flying snow made it nearly impossible to see at that speed. Zaanan squinted his eyes and looked hard.

"Oh, no!" he yelled as he fell flat.

The Snowrail entered the St. Gotthard Tunnel. In the darkness all he could do was hold on during the nine and one-half-mile trek through the tunnel. The darkness seemed to energize the bitter cold slashing of the wind. Zaanan locked his power arms in the power grip mode and rode out the darkened passageway.

After what seemed an eternity, the tunnel ended. Zaanan tried to stand up, only to find his clothes welded to the ice. Ice had formed on his hair and eyebrows and nearly frozen his face.

"Quake Mode," yelled Zaanan as his power arm discharged a severe jolt. His clothes broke free, but so did his power-grip. He swiftly slid backwards on the icy metallic surface of the train.

168

Looking back, he tried to judge the joint between car five and six. As he slid by, he missed the joint, so he continued to slide and look for the joint in cars six and seven. His rate of slide had picked up more than he realized. He misjudged the joint and missed it. He swung his arms and legs wildly, trying to grab for anything to keep him on the train. His right foot bumped something, and he stuck out his arm to catch whatever it was. It was a tail fin on the right side of the train. Zaanan reached out his right hand and grabbed it; his left hand followed. The rest of his body slid past and over the edge of the train. He looked down and his feet dangled two feet from the rail, which looked more like a blur than a rail. He looked out and saw that the Snowrail was speeding over a bridge. Hundreds of feet below were snow flocked trees. He pulled himself up on the fin and began the slow, slippery climb back to the last joint.

169

Inside the train Malcolm rested comfortably, eating a pastry and sipping a hot cup of Kaffee. All around him men and women talked casually. Some kissed or held hands. Malcolm glanced at a very old pocket watch and continued his dessert. The scenery that flashed by was breath-taking. As Malcolm sipped his Kaffee he noticed the background noises grow quiet behind him. He turned around and looked down the aisle. Two cars back stood a nearly frozen Zaanan. Everyone fell silent and still as he slowly ambled down the aisle while studying their faces.

Malcolm bolted out of his seat and spilled his Kaffee and dessert dish. Everyone looked at him, including Zaanan. Malcolm ran the other direction, cutting his way through the passengers toward the front. Zaanan grabbed a heavy coat from an empty seat and fell in behind him, dripping water as he thawed. Malcolm had to push, but Zaanan was given plenty of room. Car after car Malcolm fled until he came to the equipment car where

170

all the passengers stored their ski equipment. In the left front corner, he saw some powered tri-skis. The equipment car had a large door that could roll up into the roof of the car. Malcolm quickly pushed it up and looked out. The icy wind cut like a razor as he surveyed his situation. He leaned back into the car and jumped on a tri-ski. Zaanan reached the car just as Malcolm flew out the side of the car. Malcolm landed on all three skis and began his ride down the slopes.

"Anything he can do I can do," thought Zaanan to himself. In seconds Zaanan was zooming out the side of the Snowrail Express.

Malcolm crossed the mountain, cutting from left to right to maintain control.

"I knew I should have taken the time to learn to ski at the academy," thought Zaanan as he barreled straight down the powder white slope.

Malcolm looked back and was shocked to see Zaanan behind him. Abandoning the former ski pattern, he began to shoot straight down the mountain. The trees started to blur in front of

Malcolm. Fortunately, a heavy snow from the night before made the snow smooth and powdery. Occasionally Malcolm would make a turn to the left and then the right. If he didn't know Malcolm better Zaanan would have thought that he was being led. Malcolm jumped a bank and flew ten yards before landing. So did Zaanan who wasn't losing ground either.

Up ahead Zaanan could see what looked like a village or settlement. Malcolm was heading right for it. He skied right up the snow-covered street and plowed into a snowbank. Zaanan awkwardly brought his tri-ski to a halt without crashing this time. Malcolm helped himself out of the pile of snow. Zaanan walked over to him trying to catch his breath. The towns people came out also. Zaanan was oblivious to them, the cold or anything except Malcolm.

"Malcolm, ... you're under arrest for crimes against . . . Sphere," said Zaanan pointing his right index finger down at him.

"It worked!" yelled Malcolm, laughing out loud. "I told you
it would work." Malcolm looked at the crowd of people. He
opened his jacket collar and grabbed the skin at the base of the
neck with both hands. He peeled off the skin, which was just a
mask. The man wasn't Malcolm at all. In shock, Zaanan turned to
the crowd. There, standing in a semi-circle around Zaanan, was
a line of Troz soldiers armed with laser blasters. Zaanan glanced
around the village. Troz emblems were on buildings and clothing
everywhere. Zaanan had been lured into a Troz village hidden in
the mountains of St. Gotthard.

"Stun!" he yelled as he threw off his coat and whirled his left
power arm around at the first line of people. An electrical shock
zapped the front row and anyone touching them. They fell back
in the street. Zaanan flew to his powered tri-ski and retreated
from the village, dodging people as he slid.

"Let's get the dogs!" excitedly suggested a bearded man to the man dressed like Malcolm. He was silent for a moment as the people tried to help the ones stunned.

"I don't know - Maroth said to bring him back in one piece," said the imposter, stroking his chin. "A hunt would be fun, wouldn't it?"

"It's a great day for it!" exclaimed the man with the beard.

"Call out the dogs!" screamed the Malcolm impersonator.

In a few moments, the bearded man led a pack of dogs into the street. Women grabbed their children and ran for shelter. The dogs walked in a mechanical, awkward manner. The six dogs looked identical and even stopped together in a row. The bearded man laughed and pressed a hidden button at the base of the lead dog's head. The top of his head flipped up, revealing a programming device.

"Bring me Zaanan's coat from the ground,"

ordered the bearded man. It was promptly brought to him.
"Hold it under his nose," said the bearded man. He programmed
the dog to hunt the scent from the coat.

"Now get out of here and hide anything you have that touched
this coat."

The man who pretended to be Malcolm did as he was told.
"Hunt!" screamed the bearded man. The dogs started to run.
First, they ran to where Zaanan stood when he found out the phony Malcolm. The lead dog raised his head in a jerky, unnatural
way. The dogs had fur and looked similar to a German Shepherd.
However, their lower jaws and teeth were polished steel. Their
eyes were shiny black with a red glint in the left. Their bark was
synthetically gruff. They barked a gruff, electronic bark exactly
every eight seconds.

''They are on his trail!'' yelped the bearded man. The dogs began to run up the mountain in the very direction Zaanan had fled.

It soon became apparent to Zaanan that the tri-skis worked better with gravity than against it. The vehicle would slide backwards unless he made wide swings on the mountain side. He decided he could make it better on foot. Snow began to swirl as the wind picked up. Throwing his coat off may have added to the element of surprise in the Troz village, but now he greatly missed it. Without the sun it was difficult to get his bearings. He felt that as long as he was climbing the mountain, he was moving away from the enemy. Each step up the mountain was difficult because he sank to his knees in the snow. He knew that exerting that kind of energy without proper clothing could be deadly. The flurry changed directions.

"What's that?" he said to himself. He stopped to listen. For a second he heard nothing. Then he was certain that he had heard correctly.

"Dogs!" he said, barely able to move his pale blue lips.

Gravity seemed to give an extra nudge and he fell backwards.
He lay there a moment on his back with his boots sunk to the
knees. The slope of the mountain coupled with his fatigue made
it almost impossible to move. His body pleaded with his mind to
give up. Then he heard the dogs getting closer. He mustered the
strength to sit up. He looked around to see if the mountain could
help him. He knew it was foolish to try and out run the dogs. To
his left about thirty-five feet away he saw a jagged rock wall. It
wasn't much, but it was his only option in sight. He trudged his
way over to the wall and argued with his body to begin the climb.
The Talgent heard a bark directly behind him. He turned in time
to see the lead dog hot in pursuit. The soft snow didn't appear
to slow the dog down. He growled as he leaped at Zaanan who
only had time to raise his power arm in defense. The dog sank his
teeth into the steel metal. Zaanan saw that the dog's teeth and jaw
were metallic.

'Robots!'' he screamed. He knew he was in deep trouble as

the dog wrestled him to the ground. His only defense was to keep his power arm lodged in the dog's mouth. Up the mountain came the other five dogs followed by the villagers.

He put his right fist under the rib cage of the dog. "Stun!" he yelled.

His power arm discharged an electrical shock into the mechanical dog. Immediately it convulsed and fell backwards tumbling down the mountain about ten yards. Zaanan had hoped to conserve his power arms until absolutely needed. The other five dogs scaling the mountain made this necessary.

"Flight Mode!"

In seconds he flew up the rock wall and landed on the snow-covered ledge. The dogs reached the base of the jagged wall and sniffed where he had stood. Zaanan sat on the ledge and tried to catch his breath. His left power arm checked out undamaged. Some of the dogs pounced on the injured robot dog because Zaanan's scent was on it. Zaanan flinched as he watched them tearing it apart. One of the dogs stopped and surveyed the

problem. The red glint in his left eye scanned the area. He looked up and saw Zaanan seated on the ledge above. Zaanan didn't notice as the dog began to hunt for another way up to the ledge.

Zaanan knew he wasn't safe, but he felt he had time to regroup. He looked all around him. Above him another large ledge of ice loomed out about fifteen feet from the mountain side. It was snowing heavily, and Zaanan knew the increasing weight of the snow would soon bring the ledge crashing down on him. He noticed a cave opening just behind him in the wall. He thought that as a last resort the cave may be his only hope. However, should that ledge fall it could also be his tomb.

"There he is!" shouted a voice below him. A laser blast whizzed by him and struck the wall behind him. Zaanan looked up as a little of the ledge pelted down. He heard a loud growl to his right. In an instant he knew that one of the dogs had somehow gotten up to where he was. Without further mental debate he

dived for the cave. As he slipped in, he heard the clink of metallic
teeth near his heels. The dog stuck his large nose into the cave
and Zaanan slapped it with his right power arm. The dog began
to dig at the opening. Zaanan knew that if he used his power arms
the vibration may bring down the mountain. He didn't wait for
the dog to come to him; instead, he moved further into the mountain. The cave was only large enough to crawl through on his
hands and knees. He hadn't gone far when he came to an opening
above him. The fresh cold breeze coming down made him realize
that the hole went through to the surface. The opening was big
enough to get his shoulders through.

The dog had burrowed into the cave, forcing Zaanan to make
the decision. He had to go up to get away. He positioned himself
with his arms above his head.

"Flight Mode," he ordered.

With clenched fists he flew through the opening to the surface.

180

"Finally, something went right today," he thought to himself. He could hear the dog barking at the bottom of the cave. He could hear the villagers milling around below. He carefully walked near the ledge.

"I'm going to blow this ledge in forty seconds!" he yelled loud and clear. "Leave now and avoid the avalanche!"

The villagers took him at his word and began to flee, taking the remaining dogs with them. He decided to give them more time. Zaanan checked his power arms. His energy meter showed an ample supply of power. He switched on his homing device to alert the Sphere military to where he was. After forty-five seconds Zaanan discharged the quaking mode of his power arms into the ledge. The ridge of snow fell and slid down the mountain, but it didn't cause an avalanche. Nevertheless, he didn't fear the villagers any longer. He knew that the Troz villagers were relocating their town. He found a place out of the wind to wait for help to arrive.

Chapter Five

"How is he?" asked Kassel as he entered Asaph's room in the Medical Center.

"Kassel!" said Joseph standing to his feet.

"I came as quickly as I could," said Kassel. He walked over to the large plastic tent surrounding Asaph's bed space. Kassel was at one time a Talgent warrior for Sphere. He had been ambushed and left for dead. The Christians found him and nursed him back to health. Sphere believed him to be dead, so he remained at the Fatal Limit. He had been away for some time at another secret outpost of the Christians.

"How did it happen?" Kassel inquired.

"The man in the other tent," said Joseph, pointing at Jameston, "was apparently sent here to spy on us. He barricaded himself in the Communication Center. He was about to surrender to Asaph when his laser gun blasted a hole through to the surface."

"What are their chances?" asked Kassel.

"The doctors aren't sure. The entire space colony is praying and fasting for a miracle," said Joseph.

"Asaph looks so peaceful, doesn't he?" remarked Kassel. "Where is the spy from?"

"Zaanan says he thinks Malcolm sent him." ''Zaanan?''

"Yes, Zaanan has become a Christian."

"Well, I'll be flipped in my space boots. When did this all take place? I haven't been gone but a few weeks," said Kassel.

Kassel had talked to Zaanan about Jesus only a few weeks earlier. He was shocked and surprised to hear the news.

"Asaph always said that God has a way of making stony ground become fertile," reflected Kassel. "You mentioned Malcolm, I've been thinking about him lately. The night I was ambushed and left for dead, Malcolm was working at the assignment desk. He was a cadet at the military academy at the time. I remember being surprised to see him working the desk when I came to get my assignment. Working a meager job like that wasn't Malcolm's style. When I asked him about it, he said he was trying to learn every facet of military life. Thinking back now, I recall noticing the surveillance report was odd. It wasn't worded like the usual reports."

"So, you're thinking that Malcolm had a part in your ambush?"

"Exactly," said Kassel.

"From my recent experiences with Malcolm I don't doubt it at

184

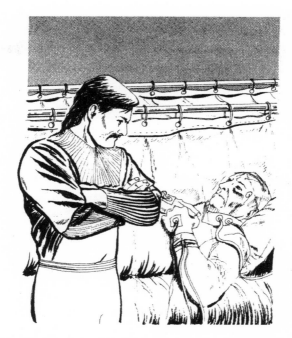

all," interjected Joseph. "Zaanan has gone after Malcolm."

"Who sent him?" asked Kassel, "Did he finish the basic discipleship course?"

"No," said Joseph sadly. "Zaanan left in a bitter, vengeful mood to look for Malcolm."

"You better add him to your prayer list," observed Kassel.

"Joseph," said Asaph weakly.

"Yes sir, I'm here." Joseph leaned on the translucent tent to get closer.

"Must for ... give," said Asaph struggling to speak. "I ... for ... give."

Asaph lapsed back into a semi-conscious state. Joseph stood frozen by the tent for a moment.

"What did ... he say?" said a muffled voice. It was Jameston. He was also terribly ill from the radiation. The effects from exposure were worse on Asaph because of his advanced age.

Joseph walked over to Jameston's tent. "He said he forgives you," Joseph said after staring at him for a moment.

Jameston wasn't strong enough to get up, but he turned his

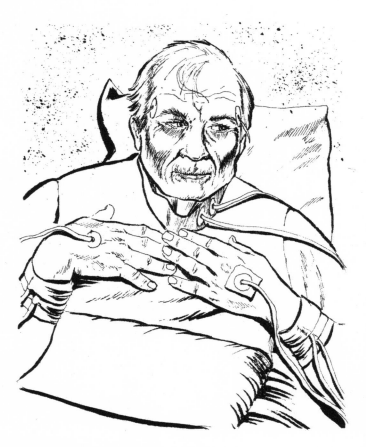

head and cut his eyes toward Asaph.

"Thank you," he said, "How are my babies?" Joseph's anger welled up within him. He saw Jameston as an awful madman, a man who foolishly harmed the most important man in Christendom at that time. Joseph wasn't at the point of forgiving.

Chapter Six

Zaanan sat wrapped in towels and blankets trying to thaw out. He sipped on a warm beverage and periodically turned his body so all areas could be near the fire.

"Our search team just called in from where you said the village was," informed the officer that Zaanan had met when he first arrived. "Just as you suspected, they have moved, leaving little behind."

Zaanan reshuffled his covers and stared straight ahead deep in thought. The officer stood still for a moment thinking Zaanan was about to say something. When it was apparent, he wasn't, the officer poured himself some hot tea.

"Maroth planned it all in order to catch me," mused Zaanan. "How did Maroth know that Malcolm is a fugitive or that I'd even come after him?"

The officer could tell that Zaanan was talking to himself. Zaanan sat for a long time reliving every moment, every word, trying to look for clues in a bizarre circumstance. Zaanan's thoughts were interrupted by a call from the headquarters of the City of Sphere.

"Supreme Calvert Van Hensen," said the officer. He snapped to attention as the Calvert came into view on the visual communicator. The Swiss officer had never been so close to a Supreme Calvert.

"Where is Talgent Zaanan?"

"He is here, sir. I'll get him, sir," said the officer as formally as possible. The few workers in the office stopped their duties and

tried to watch what was going on.

"Yes, sir. This is Zaanan," said the Talgent in a much less formal manner.

"What is that you're involved in?"

"It's kind of a long story," replied Zaanan.

"Did you find Malcolm there in the Alps?" asked the Calvert.

"No sir, this Malcolm turned out to be an impostor."

"Oh . . . well that makes what I have to say a little less crazy sounding," said the Calvert. "We now have five places where Malcolm is reported to be."

Zaanan said nothing at first. He felt exhausted at the thought of possibly reliving the recent past five more times.

"You look somewhat tired; are you?" asked Van Hensen.

"A little," responded Zaanan. "This place turned out to be a trap set for me."

"Well then, we'll send out units to these five places and check them out."

189

"Wait a moment," requested Zaanan. "I'm not sure how Malcolm is linked to Maroth, but there does seem to be something to it. I have a funny feeling that Malcolm really is at one of these places. I think he expects me to figure it out and come. Where are the locations?"

"Do you think it's wise to go?"

"Yes, sir. It's the only way to get Malcolm. It may even open the door to capturing Maroth and defusing Troz."

"Well, one is in the Northwest region of Sector A-25," started Van Hensen.

"Never. It's apparent that Malcolm doesn't like cold weather."

"How about Sector H-2?"

"I don't think so."

"Sector N-22?"

"Isn't that a group of islands in the Quilldian Sea?" asked Zaanan.

"Yes, I believe it is," answered the Calvert.

"That's where I'll find Malcolm waiting for me."

"Are you sure?"

"If anyone in the world knows Malcolm, I do."

"If you like, I can assign another Talgent to assist."

"No sir. Malcolm is waiting for me alone. Anyone coming along would force him to prolong the inevitable."

"When can you leave?"

"As soon as my feet thaw."

Chapter Seven

Once in the air again Zaanan felt better. He set his course and sat back for the ride. Starjets were incredible crafts with awesome potential. Zaanan knew that Malcolm would be somewhere on one of those islands. He knew because no other location had any significance in the chain that linked Zaanan to Malcolm.

As he soared thousands of feet above the earth, his mind drifted back to a time before he was a Talgent. Zaanan and Malcolm were at the top of their class at the academy. News came that Talgent Kassel had perished in the line of duty. A replacement was to be selected from the cadets. Zaanan, Malcolm and a

cadet named Byn-Alford were chosen for the contest. The three of them were equipped with a videotaping device to record their every move. They were to travel to a string of remote islands. There they were to recover the Opal of OPARA. Each was tested independently; then they were tested as a group.

They made it to the island of OPARA and without problem they recovered the Opal. The OP ARA beaches were quite unique. A sand beach stretched one hundred yards between a twenty- foot rock wall and the ocean. The giant walls had been built long ago. They were crumbling in sections and covered in vines. The three cadets had easily scaled the wall going in and repelled back down it when leaving. The young men were confident of their victory and disappointed at the ease of their exercise. As they ran across the long beach area, a giant round cage came flying up from down the beach. The cage ball was the island's sentry system. It swooped down, opened what looked like

a mouth, scooped up Byn-Alford and flew on down the beach. Zaanan and Malcolm stood there for a moment undecided as to what they should do. Zaanan felt they should rescue Byn-Alford. Malcolm said that since they had been spotted, they should run for it and get the Opal back to Sphere.

Zaanan decided to go back for Byn-Alford even though reason said to flee. Malcolm headed for the ocean and Zaanan, the wall. Once again Zaanan easily entered the City of OPARA. The ease of getting around bothered him. He had been careful enough and yet no one seemed terribly insecure as he watched from a hiding place. From the maps he had received before coming he determined where the jail was. He passed by the royal court where they had stolen the Opal. As he hurried through the court area, he heard people coming. Zaanan quickly hid as three men formally marched in single file. The lead man was ceremonially dressed and carried a spear. The man walking in the rear of the

line was dressed the same and also carried a spear. The difference
in the two men was that the latter marched backwards. The dress
of the man in the middle indicated that he was royalty or a priest.
He was carrying a plushly decorated pillow with something on it.
The group marched to a giant granite statue of a tiger, the same
tiger from which Zaanan, Malcolm and Byn-Alford had taken
the Opal of OPARA. The guards turned and stood, straining their
eyes to see any intruder while the priest reinserted the opal eye.
Zaanan quickly hid so as not to be spotted. The strange ceremo-
ny put a different light on the seeming success of their mission,
which apparently wasn't over. The opal they had originally taken
must have been a phony. Now it made sense to him; he knew that
it had gone far too easily. The islanders must have guessed their
intent and switched the real opal with a phony. When the cage
ball captured Byn-Alford, they must have thought that Zaanan
and Malcolm fled the island. When the people left Zaanan moved

on and set Byn-Alford free. Next, he grabbed the real Opal of OPARA and the two left the island. Back at headquarters the video recordings were reviewed from each cadet. Zaanan was clearly chosen as the winner. Malcolm became greatly disturbed by their choice. Malcolm was so bitter that it severed their lifelong friendship. Malcolm left the academy and joined the SSP.

As Zaanan sat in his starjet alone with his thoughts, his eyes fell on the Stone, the one that Joseph had dropped into his cockpit back at the Fatal Limit. He reached down and picked it up. For days he had tried to push God out of his thoughts without success. He had attempted to turn away from his decision to follow Christ, but he couldn't.

"What was the chapter Joseph told me to listen to?" Zaanan asked himself.

"Matthew ... Matthew eighteen," he finally said after searching his memory.

He made a fist around the Stone and said, "Matthew eighteen."

The Stone quickly began reciting the verses of Matthew eighteen. Zaanan's skeleton was used as the amplifier to his eardrum. Zaanan listened intently to the first twenty verses. He felt that some applied to the things he and his brother had spoken about. However, verse twenty-one caught his attention.

"Then Peter came to Jesus and asked, 'Lord, how many times shall I forgive my brother when he sins against me? Up to seven times?'

"Jesus answered, 'I tell you, not seven times, but seventy times seven.' "

"That's - four hundred and ninety times," thought Zaanan. Zaanan listened as the Stone quoted the story about a king who wanted to settle accounts with his servants. A man came forth who owed the king several million dollars. The man was unable to pay his debt so the king ordered that he, his wife, children, and

all he owned be sold in payment. The servant fell to his knees and begged to be given more time. The king took pity on the man and canceled his debt.

The servant left a free man. However, on his way home he met a man who owed him just a few dollars. The servant demanded payment. The man fell to his knees begging for more time. The servant refused and had the man imprisoned.

Some servants of the king saw what happened and reported it to the king. The king called in the unmerciful servant. The king chided the servant saying that since the king forgave so much, he should be willing to forgive a little. The king had the wicked servant jailed.

The Stone recited verse thirty-five in conclusion:

"This is how my heavenly Father will treat each of you unless you forgive your brother from your heart."

Zaanan relaxed his grip on the Stone. He had learned in his

198

short time at the Fatal Limit how to look for personal application from the scripture. He thought about the debt of sin he owed God. God could have said it was time to pay up. Zaanan asked for God's forgiveness. God the Father had already sent His own Son, Jesus Christ, to die and pay for Zaanan's sin debt. Zaanan saw himself forgiven, but then he was faced with Malcolm, a man who had done many wrongs to him and the people he cared for. Zaanan had kept a mental list of the wrongs Malcolm had done. Zaanan felt this list served to justify his anger and bitterness. When Zaanan began to compare his own sin against God with Malcolm's sin against him, God truly had forgiven the most. If God could forgive, surely Zaanan could. Zaanan realized that he had been imprisoned by his bitterness toward Malcolm.

"Father," prayed Zaanan, "I agree with You that my bitterness toward Malcolm is wrong. I confess that I hate the things he's done to me and the people I love. Father I - forgive Malcolm with

my mind, help me forgive him from my heart. Please set my spirit free. In Jesus name I pray. Amen."

Zaanan sensed a change. He felt lighter and relaxed. The joy he experienced at the Fatal Limit returned. Zaanan was still looking forward to seeing Malcolm but for very different reasons.

Chapter Eight

Zaanan's instruments indicated that he was approaching Sector N-22 in the Quilldian Sea. He slowed down his craft. He instructed his instruments to locate anyone bearing the Sphere emblem. At birth, all babies born in Sphere were tatooed with the Sphere insignia. In the tatoo dye was a special metallic dust that could help track a citizen.

Zaanan flew over several small islands at about fifty feet off the ground. As he came up on one of the larger islands, his scanner indicated a bleep. Then a second bleep registered and disappeared.

The first bleep remained and grew in intensity. Zaanan switched on his outside viewer. There standing on the beach with his shoulders squared and his hands on his hips was Malcolm. Zaanan knew in his heart it was the real Malcolm. Zaanan circled back around and landed in the jungle not far from Malcolm. Zaanan removed his flight suit and debated about wearing his power arms. He decided to wear them just in case. In just a matter of minutes Zaanan was outside his craft heading for Malcolm. As he came into the clearing, he saw Malcolm facing him about twenty-five yards away.

"I was beginning to think you wouldn't come," yelled Malcolm.

"Malcolm, you are under arrest for multiple crimes against Sphere," stated Zaanan.

Malcolm laughed as Zaanan grew closer.

"Does this place bring back memories?" asked Malcolm in a sarcastic manner.

"Come with me peacefully, old friend."

"Old friend? You have a short memory. I've been trying to kill you for a long time."

Zaanan didn't reply. He stopped walking toward Malcolm just in case Malcolm had set some kind of trap.

"Have you ever wondered which one of us really was the best suited for the rank of Talgent?" asked Malcolm.

"Sphere decided I was."

"You got the real opal by pure luck and you know it," snapped Malcolm. "It's just the two of us here. Why don't you take off those power arms, and we'll settle this once and for all."

"I don't want to fight you, Malcolm. You're the best friend I ever had."

"Best friend? Za, I stopped being your friend a long time ago."

"I know you've done a lot of things to prove that but I want you to know that I - forgive you."

"Forgive me! I don't want to be forgiven, I want your head!"

shouted Malcolm, visibly angry.

"Come on, Malcolm, let's go."

"I'll come peacefully if you can take me without your power arms. Unless you feel you really can't."

Zaanan knew that Malcolm was goading him, but he felt that this would be their only chance to settle this once and for all. Zaanan carefully released and removed his power arms. Malcolm almost giggled with excitement at the possibility.

"All right, Malcolm, it's your move." The two moved closer together and slowly circled each other. Malcolm made the first move. They locked bodies and tried to wrestle each other to the ground. Malcolm pulled free his left arm and punched Zaanan in the stomach. Zaanan fell back to the ground, short of breath. He had forgotten how strong Malcolm was. Malcolm stood reveling in the moment. Suddenly Malcolm grabbed his own neck. He

staggered and fell face down in the sand. Zaanan ran to his side and rolled him over onto his back.

"Malcolm, are you ... "

Zaanan felt a pinch in his own neck and everything turned a dark greenish black.

Chapter Nine

Splash!

Zaanan tingled as he felt he had been hit by water. He opened his eyes and everything was a blur. He could see images but not faces. He heard men talking but their voices were slow and deep. He couldn't make out anything they said. Next, he felt a swift kick in his side. He knew he had been kicked hard but without feeling any pain. Everything faded to black.

Zaanan had a terrible nightmare. Nothing about the dream made sense. Lights, colors and sounds flashed, whirled and melted. He saw faces of people of all different sizes. Some shattered

like glass as others turned into puddles of water. Zaanan sensed himself running in slow motion to lock a door. Just as he reached it, the door opened, and a great suction began pulling him toward outer space. He fell to the floor and tried to crawl against the wind. Objects flew past him and out the door. The force dragged him out of the door, and he fell down, down, and down toward an abyss.

"No!" he yelled as he sat up. Perspiration ran down his face and dripped from his chin. He realized his feet and hands were tied.

"You had some terrible dream," said Malcolm from across the room.

Zaanan looked around. He was a prisoner in a hut made of woven palm branches and tree limbs.

"Where are we?" asked Zaanan.

"That's a good question," retorted Malcolm. A door on the

hut opened. Four men came in. They wore large earrings and a feathered necklace. They had cloths wrapped around their waists and tied, resembling diapers. They marched in and pulled Zaanan and Malcolm to their feet. Zaanan's head pounded so hard he could hear his heart beating. Taking a knife, they cut the ropes around their feet. Then they pulled their captives outside the tent. They marched them through what looked like a village of men, women, and children. At the far end of the village Zaanan could see a little man outfitted in colorful clothes and an enormous headdress. He was seated with about ten people standing around him dressed like Zaanan 's escorts. When they got about ten feet away their guards tripped them. Zaanan fell but was able to break his fall with his hands.

"We're in trouble," said Malcolm, spitting sand out of his mouth.

"Silence!" cried a voice in the same language Malcolm spoke.

208

Zaanan raised his head and saw a white man standing to the right of the chief. He was dressed like the chief, but he held an elaborately decorated wand. He waved it from left to right in front of Zaanan and Malcolm. Their guards grabbed them by the hair and pulled them until they stood up. The white man walked over and stood directly in front of them.

"Sphere ... it's been a long time since I uttered that horrible word. My name was Tate at one time. Now I'm known as Dun-Tu. I'm the chief's assistant."

"What brought you here?" asked Zaanan.

"Oh, a love for the ocean and a hate for computers," answered Tate.

A woman came running through the crowd; she pushed past the guards and hurried up to the chief. In her native tongue she excitedly spoke with him. He rose from his seat and everyone

209

bowed their heads.

"What's the problem?" asked Malcolm.

"The chief's daughter has been very ill. The woman said she felt the child is at the point of death. It looks like your deaths may be postponed a while." assured Tates.

"'Tell the chief I can help her," offered Zaanan.

"What can you do?" asked Tate.

"I ... I believe in the power of prayer."

"What?" said Malcolm in a loud whisper.

"I believe that nothing is impossible with God, " continued Zaanan, ignoring Malcolm's disbelief.

"'That sounds a little unusual coming from a Talgent warrior," wondered Tate.

"Zaanan believes in God. How about that!" mused Malcolm. "Why did you come to arrest me for alien-thought?"

"I'll mention your beliefs to the chief, " said Tate. He walked

off and followed the chief to his tent. Zaanan noticed that the sky was gray and the wind was picking up.

In a few minutes Tate emerged from the chief's tent. He ordered Zaanan's guard to bring him to the tent. Tate stopped Zaanan at the door of the tent.

"If she lives, you live," Tate stated without any emotion in his voice.

Zaanan entered the tent. It was full of people. They moved back to clear a path to the girl for Zaanan. She was a beautiful, frail child who appeared to be asleep on a cot. Her mother wiped her feverish brow with a damp cloth. The chief stood at the head of her bed. Zaanan had never prayed for anyone to be healed. He didn't really know what to say. He walked over to her bed and knelt beside her. His hands were still tied as he placed them on her cot. He rested his brow on his hands and prayed out loud.

211

"Father, in the name of Jesus Christ, I ask You to heal this girl. Amen."

This was his prayer. Everyone seemed somewhat disappointed. Zaanan looked at the girl, who remained asleep and feverish. His guards led Zaanan back to his tent and tied his feet again.

"Well?" asked Malcolm.

"I don't know," answered Zaanan, "it's out of my hands now."

"That's wonderful news," snapped Malcolm. "Well, what's your plan?"

"That was my plan."

"That's wonderful," said Malcolm. "In a little while they're going to figure out you were just buying time and they're going to come for us."

Zaanan said nothing as he continued to pray under his breath. Outside the wind was blowing harder.

After about three hours the guards returned.

"I don't think they're happy," jabbed Malcolm.

The guards went through the same routine as before. They cut the ropes on their feet and led them out to the chief. Tate walked over to them.

"The chief's daughter is still near death," said Tate. "He feels your time is up."

The chief stood and raised his arms above his head. He shouted something in the language of the islands. The natives cheered and danced around.

"I don't think that they are going to give you the Medallion of Valor," spurred Malcolm. The natives pranced all around them. Their guards grabbed their hands and pulled them to the edge of a large hole in the ground. The hole was about twenty feet across. Long bamboo poles were lowered down into the pit. Four-inch vertical holes had been cut into the bamboo poles. The holes

213

were about eighteen inches apart. A person climbed the pole by
using their hands and big toes.

The guards took the ropes from Zaanan and Malcolm and led
them down into the deep pit.

"Malcolm, look at the clouds," observed Zaanan. The clouds out
over the ocean looked dark and angry. The wind had increased
in force all during the day. Malcolm looked up for a moment but
said nothing. Tate followed the group down into the pit. At the
bottom two guards held spears to the backs of Zaanan and Malcolm as two other guards freed their hands. Next a guard tied one
end of a grass rope to Zaanan's left wrist. The other end of the
rope was attached to Malcolm's left wrist. The rope allowed them
to stand apart about eight feet.

"When given the signal you are to fight to the death," stated Tate
plainly. Tate was the last to climb out of the pit. The bamboo

poles were removed. Tate raised a seashell to his lips and blew. The crowd went wild in celebration.

Zaanan and Malcolm looked up to the surface. Faces crowded around the opening and jeered down on the men. The chief walked to the edge of the hole and threw a large knife in. Zaanan and Malcolm jumped back to avoid being hit. The knife stuck straight up in the dirt floor.

"Malcolm, we don't have to do this. We don't have to fight," urged Zaanan.

"Are you kidding? This is my chance," sneered Malcolm.

"Let's join together against them as we once would have," argued Zaanan.

"That was too long ago."

"Not in my heart."

The noise from above was deafening as they challenged them to fight. The crowd was hungry for blood.

215

"Your religion has made you soft, Talgent Zaanan," sneered Malcolm.

Malcolm jumped for the knife and grabbed it. Zaanan instinctively took a defensive posture. The crowd shouted even louder. Malcolm lunged at Zaanan and laughed. Zaanan stepped back as far as their rope allowed him. Once again, they were linked together in life.

A large clap of thunder broke the crowd's fiendish concentration. The gusty wind blew down one of the villager's hut. The women began to gather the children and move them to safety.

Down in the pit Zaanan continued to avoid the jabs of Malcolm. Malcolm lunged and Zaanan's footing slipped in the dirt. Malcolm grabbed him and tried to stab Zaanan in the chest. Zaanan grasped Malcolm's wrist with both his hands and kept the knife from drawing blood. The two stood struggling over the knife. Malcolm put his other hand in Zaanan's face and pushed back his head. Zaanan bit his fingers. Malcolm screamed. Zaanan whirled around and flipped Malcolm over his shoulder. Malcolm raised up and Zaanan hit him in the mouth with his right

216

fist. The knife flew out of his hand and landed near the wall of the pit. Zaanan ran for the knife but Malcolm pulled hard on the rope. Zaanan fell face down. Malcolm made his bid to regain the knife but Zaanan grabbed his foot and tripped him. The two men locked bodies and rolled around the pit fighting. Malcolm locked his arm around Zaanan's neck and began to choke him with all his might. Using his elbow, Zaanan jabbed Malcolm in the ribs until he let go. Zaanan pushed Malcolm and dove for the knife. In an instant Zaanan had it. Malcolm cautiously stood to his feet. Zaanan took the knife and hurled it out the top of the pit. The crowd jumped back for a moment but quickly returned.

The wind blew increasingly stronger. Rain began to come down in sheets. The pit must have been some sort of rain collecting tank. Water flowed in from an unnoticed opening in the wall of the pit. The crowd above began to chant. The slogan grew in intensity until Zaanan and Malcolm looked up.

''Cada-Maylon, Cada-Maylon, Cada-Maylon,'' they cried.

"What's Cada-Maylon?" asked Malcolm.

"It's what this sector was once called," shouted Zaanan to be

heard above the noise. "It means 'island of the panther.' "

Behind them they heard a growl. Zaanan and Malcolm whirled around. A large panther emerged from the opening in the wall. He had been released into the tunnel that led to the opening. The men froze in their tracks.

On the surface the natives were met with a surprise of their own. The storm had intensified into a typhoon. The king and Tate ran for their tents. The other villagers scattered in all directions looking for their families and shelter. The rain and wind were now almost blinding. Water was now gushing into the pit.

The panther lunged for Zaanan. He wedged his forearm as deep as he could into the back of the panther's mouth. The panther knocked him over into the knee-deep water and tried to claw him. In an instant Malcolm jumped on the panther's back and wrapped his rope around the cat's throat. He choked with all his might. The panther gagged and coughed. He reared up off of Zaanan and tried to throw Malcolm. The water was gushing in so fast that the rocks around the opening began to give way.

Zaanan struggled to his feet as the water reached his waist. Malcolm tenaciously held onto his choke hold as the cat tried to unsaddle him. The thrashing about of the cat kept pulling Zaanan off balance because the rope held the men together. He jumped on the panther's head.

"Hold him under," he yelled above the storm.

Malcolm helped him hold the panther as it fought to stay above water. The water level was now at their chest.

"I think we can let go now," shouted Malcolm. "He should leave us alone."

"When I count three, jump back," ordered Zaanan. "One ... two ... THREE!"

Malcolm and Zaanan let go and swam away. The panther began to tread water and concentrated on survival. The water had risen to their shoulders.

"Got any ideas?" shouted Zaanan.

"None," answered Malcolm.

Even if they could tread the water until it reached the top Zaanan was certain the sides would collapse if the water got much higher. The walls of the pit were too slippery to climb. Even if they stood on each other's shoulders the pit was too deep.

219

Zaanan looked over at Malcolm. He could see in Malcolm's eyes that he had come to the same conclusion. Both men joined the panther in treading water. The big cat nervously swam from wall to wall trying to find an exit. The rope between Zaanan and Malcolm made it difficult to stay afloat as the water inched up.

Almost as if from heaven, two bamboo poles entered the water beside Zaanan and Malcolm. Zaanan looked up and saw the chief and Tate struggling against the typhoon winds to help them. Malcolm quickly started up the ladder one big toe at a time.

"Wait, we can't leave the panther here!" screamed Zaanan.

"Are you crazy?"

"Come on, help me!"

Malcolm looked at Zaanan as if it were against his better judgment. He jumped back into the pit. They cornered the cat and Zaanan circled around him. The panther was too tired to offer much resistance. Malcolm was on the panther's left side and Zaanan his right. They made sure the rope was firmly under the cat's shoulders.

"Hurry!" yelled Tate.

The men repositioned the poles and began to slowly climb toe over toe to the mouth of the pit. Tate and the chief helped lift the panther out of the hole. The cat scrambled to get free and ran to safety. Malcolm and Zaanan fell to the ground on their hands and knees. Both men were terribly exhausted. The chief knelt beside Zaanan and bowed before him. The rain and wind made it difficult to see or hear. Tate got right next to Zaanan's left ear and yelled.

''The chief's daughter is healed!''

Zaanan sat there in amazement.

"We must get to shelter quickly!" urged Tate. The chief and Tate helped Zaanan to his feet.

"Wait - where's Malcolm?" screamed Zaanan. The three men turned around, but Malcolm was gone.

"Quickly! Quickly!" pleaded Tate.

Zaanan reluctantly gave in and followed the chief. The storm grew worse by the moment. Carefully they inched their way toward the other side of the island. Soon they joined the rest of the tribe in a large cave. There they huddled close until the typhoon passed.

Chapter Ten

The next day the sky was clear except for a few clouds edging out of the horizon. Slowly the villagers began rambling through the wreckage from the storm. Zaanan had spent most of the night concerned about his starjet and Malcolm. He now stood on a cliff overlooking the devastated island. Palm trees were uprooted and splintered. Expired sea life and seaweed covered the beach. The ocean churned below him in an array of colors.

"We will build back," informed Tate climbing up beside Zaanan on the cliff.

"How is the chief's daughter?"

"She is even better today," replied Tate. "How did you heal her?"

"I didn't," said Zaanan. "I asked God to heal her."

"How can I find out about this God?"

Zaanan reached in his pocket and took out his Stone. He handed it to Tate.

"Make a fist around it and ask it any question you have. It will tell you all about God and His son, Jesus Christ. I'll let you keep it if you promise to share what you learn with your chief and the villagers."

"Gladly," answered Tate studying the Stone. "But this is your Stone."

"I know where I can get another one," said Zaanan smiling. "Well, I'm going to find what's left of my starjet."

Zaanan started to walk down the small hill to the beach.

"Oh - Zaanan," called Tate, "your starjet is fine. We took it to a safe place when you were unconscious. We thought you were going to die so we decided to keep it."

Zaanan stood still a moment.

"Of course, I'm very happy you are alive," said Tate with a sheepish grin. "Come, I'll take you to it."

223

They walked along, climbing over downed trees, and pushing debris aside.

"Do you think Malcolm escaped?" asked Zaanan. "To be honest, I don't think so," assured Tate, "not in that storm. In fact, I'm sure he's dead."

''With Malcolm no one can be sure of anything,'' thought Zaanan to himself.

Later that afternoon Zaanan blasted off in his starjet headed for home. He circled the island once with his scanner switched on. He detected only one bleep on his scanner. He knew that Tate had a Sphere tatoo so he felt assured that Malcolm was no longer on the island. He turned his starjet toward the City of Sphere.

As he soared across the sky, he reflected about his time on Cada-Maylon. He marveled at the power of God to heal that young girl. He honestly felt no bitterness anymore toward Malcolm. In the silence of space Zaanan's thoughts drifted to the Fatal Limit. He thought of Asaph lying there so close to death. Asaph had come to mean a great deal to him. His heart reached out to his father recovering from the stroke. He pondered his childhood

dream of being united as a family. He envisioned himself seated at a banquet table in the Fatal Limit sharing a feast with his brother, mother and father. He couldn't help but cry.

Thousands of miles away in the Fatal Limit a group of weary prayer warriors kept up an earnest
vigil. The space colony's night cycle was coming to an end. Joseph was sitting beside the tent of Asaph, asleep. Allison was sleeping in a chair just outside the door of Asaph's room. A doctor quietly checked the computer read-out connected to Jameston's tent.

Asaph quietly sat up in bed.

"Yes Lord, he said. "Of course, I'm ready."

The doctor heard a noise and turned toward
Asaph's bed. He was surprised to see Asaph sitting up and talking.

"Joseph," he whispered as he nudged Joseph from his sleep. Joseph sat up and instantly noticed the change in Asaph.

225

"Allison," called Joseph out loud. Everyone in the room woke up, including Jameston.

"Look at his face," marveled Allison as she joined Joseph beside his tent.

"There's a glow ... no, a glory about it," said Joseph. They couldn't understand every word that Asaph was saying. His tired wrinkled eyes twinkled with delight. He smiled, laughed and sometimes appeared to listen. His gaze was fixed on something at the foot of his bed. Asaph seemed to be unaware that Joseph and Allison stood beside him.

"It's beautiful," Asaph declared, "more beautiful than I ever dreamed!"

His eyes shined in the dimly lit room.

"Yes, I'm ready," he said. Asaph slowly stretched his arms out and up toward the foot of the bed. Joseph noticed his right hand closed in a fist. Asaph smiled. Then the glow on his face left. He closed his eyes and gently laid back on his bed. His body went limp. His right fist opened, and his Stone rolled out of his hand onto his bed. Joseph's eyes widened.

"Look, Asaph has been holding the Stone in his hand since the night he was exposed to radiation," said Joseph. "He's been listening to the scripture the entire time."

By this time, the room was filled with doctors and friends. Joseph and Allison embraced and cried on each other's shoulders.

After a while Joseph walked over to Jameston's tent. Jameston lay motionless, staring at the ceiling.

"Is he gone?" asked Jameston.

"Yes," replied Joseph softly.

"Do you think he forgave me?"

"Yes ... I do."

"Do you forgive me?"

"Yes ... I do," answered Joseph after a long pause.

"How do you die?" asked Jameston.

"Men die as they lived."

"Tell me how to live like Asaph."

Artificial sunlight dawned as the day cycle began in the space colony. The Christians carried on their mission in the Fatal Limit and throughout the universe. The existence of mankind had always been fragile, and this day was no different. Christianity had survived the three thousand years since the death and resurrection of Christ. No matter how difficult the times became Christianity lived on for one simple reason:

"Jesus Christ is the same yesterday and today and forever."
Hebrews 13:8

EPILOGUE

Truth empowers. Truth sets people free. Truth offers the only real path to genuine determination and lasting progress. Falsehood is a crooked and an uneven snake that only pretends to be a road.

Sphere endeavored to retain power and influence on mankind by constantly changing the rules. It kept people off-balance and insecure. Sphere as a global authority continually screamed that truth was falsehood -- a mirage.

Without explanation to anyone, Malcolm was forgiven by Sphere and reinstated as head of the Sphere Secret Police. The Sphere had its reasons. Fairness or justice was a line drawn in sand not chiseled in stone. It didn't seem that Sphere knew that Malcolm was also the leader of Troz the largest terrorist group on and off planet. Or did the Sphere know? Sphere decided he was of use and that was enough. Could the Sphere trust him? The Sphere trusted no one.

Daily schedules in the City of Sphere went from two work cylces to three. Eight hours for work, eight hours for sleep, and eight hours for pleasure with each requiring a detailed audible report in a Chron device. The change was thought to be a gift by the citizens. But, a relaxed mind wanders. It was just more cheese for the mousetrap.

Sphere also knew that given time, people infected with alien-thought and scattered into hiding would begin to feel confident and safe. Confident and safe enough to come out of hiding. The Sphere would be there ready and waiting.

Did the Sphere government know of Zaanan's conversion to Christianity? Time would tell.

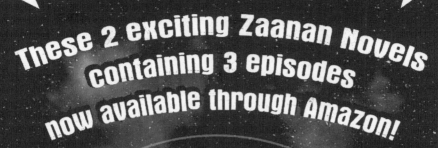

About the Author and Illustrator

Al Bohl is an American author, illustrator and filmmaker.
There are five episodes in the Zaanan series.
He resides in Bossier City, LA with his wife Doris. You may
contact him through his email account al@albohl.com.
Put the word "Zaanan" in the subject heading.

Made in the USA
Columbia, SC
23 September 2024

42932076R00138